ROCK BAND FIGHTS EVIL #6

THE GOOD SON

ROCK BAND FIGHTS EVIL #6

THE GOOD SON

D.J. Butler

WordFire Press
Colorado Springs, Colorado

Chapter One

The Ruins of Ainok and the Gate of Hell

THE END OF THE AGE OF PISCES

When life gives you lemons …"

The fairy Twitch stood surveying the horde of champing, snarling enemies on their heels. Queen Mab, the hideous Belial with beak and tentacles snapping, and the Legate of Heaven, that conniving old weasel, stood at the head of the wild hunt. Behind them, Queen's Rangers fidgeted, Wild Things bellowed and roared, and demons of Hell raged. A cloud of swarming Zvuvim buzzed all about them, almost obscuring the shroud of mist from which the pursuers and pursued had all emerged in a pell-mell race from the Crossroads of Rahab and Mab's own Queendom. A white glow among the giant flies might have marked the presence of Raphael, the renegade Bearer of the Word.

Behind Jim was the open gate of Hell and its doorkeeper, Baraqyel. Around him, almost unrecognizable after millennia of decay, were the ruins of his birthplace: Ainok, City of the Free. Beside him were, if he could be said to possess any such thing, his friends. His *surviving* friends. Also Jane, who had been Qayna, who had killed Jim once, and the flesh-eating horse she rode.

For all the crowd and the chaos, he felt profoundly alone.

Monsters in front and monsters behind. Things were about to get crazy.

Check that; things had been crazy for a long, long time.

"I don't actually know how the saying ends." The fairy's voice was strained. It had taken a real beating in Kansas City and in the Queendom, and it looked like it was barely still on its feet. "I never heard him finish it."

"Lemonade." Mike supplied the deficit. "You make lemonade."

"Yeah," Eddie grunted. "Only life hasn't handed us anything as nice as a lemon. And precious few people want to drink a tall, cold glass of shit." Eddie held his shotgun and Jim's father's hoof clipping. He hadn't offered the hoof back to Jim after recovering it from Mab.

Maybe he didn't trust Jim anymore.

Probably he shouldn't. Still, Eddie and the others had rescued Jim from Mab's Baobab-root prison cell and fought through to successfully carry out Jim's plan of crossing to Hell under the feet of Rahab the Dragon. They'd done it at the cost of Adrian Pew's life.

Maybe that was the moment when Jim had lost Eddie's trust.

"The Council sits." Baraqyel the Fallen called out over Jim's head at the army before him. Jim didn't look back, but he heard rustling and scrabbling sounds that had to be the mustering of Hell's defenses. "Will you join the other Princes, my lord Belial?"

Belial surged forward. He was more like a plant or a squid than anything humanoid; he'd been more radical than many of his fellows when they had begun altering themselves. Not that Jim had been there to see it, but he'd heard the stories. Belial had been one of the first to join Jim's father in the experiment and one of the least restrained.

He'd wanted power, he'd taken a great risk, and he'd paid a serious price. He looked more like a talking, tentacled avocado-worm with a beak than like the angel he'd once been. That beak and those tentacles had tortured Jim through many a fragmented dream.

"I will!" Belial's voice rang like twisting steel in the reddish-black gloom of the ruins of Ainok. He drew himself up to his full height, towering even over Baraqyel, who was several times the height of a man. "Stand aside."

Jim tightened his grip on his sword and ventured a look back. A thing like an enormous toad squatted immediately behind him, claws dug into the stony ground. Its maw gaped open, mephitic fumes rising from the rotting flesh of its tongue. It had to stand with its mouth open, though—the creature, one of the thousand nameless demon-things of Hell, had every one of its hundred unblinking eyes embedded in the slimy gray meat of its uvula. Behind the toad waited others of his father's minions, implacable, ready.

"Certainly, my lord." Baraqyel didn't blink, but the doorkeeper did keep the point of his spear angling generally in Belial's direction, poised to defend if he had to. "Dismiss your armies, and you are welcome to take your seat."

"Armies?" Belial shook as he laughed, a horrible, rumbling sound with wet tearing noises within it. "These are my friends."

"As you say, my lord. But your friends have no right to sit in the Council, unless they are invited in by carried motion."

"And the whelp?" Mab demanded. She held a spear, too, shaped like a lightning bolt. Slow, plodding *booms* in the distance reminded Jim that the great defender of her Queendom, the Baobab Tree, was free and mobile. From the sound of the booms, it might be coming this way.

At least Rahab was chained.

Jim smelled brimstone. A Hellhound. He almost smiled, and wondered if it was Phthonos again. The mindless affection of his father's hounds was almost enough to ease his sense of solitude. Almost.

"The whelp has a right to be here," Jim said. He gestured expansively at the tumbled megaliths, the rubble, the crater, and the lake with the dead birds floating in it. "This is the whelp's home."

His eye fixed inadvertently on the lone visible star in the sky, and he had to tear it away.

"Whether he appreciates it or not," Baraqyel said smoothly, and Jim remembered that he had offended the gatekeeper at their last meeting.

"And your friends?" Mab stared at Jim with fire in her eyes. "Will you leave them here to entertain us?"

"I got a right!" Eddie waved Azazel's hoof in his left hand.

Belial's tentacles tightened in unison around an imaginary cone pointing in Eddie's direction. The monstrous Prince of Hell had no discernible eyes, but he seemed nevertheless to be looking quizzically at Eddie. "*Do* you?"

Eddie held the shotgun by the pump in his other hand, and with one quick motion he shook it up and down. The ejected spent shell clattered across the stone and plopped into dead water. "And I got a counterargument for anyone who disagrees."

"Attack!" Belial howled, and surged forward.

In a burst of sulfuric flame, the Hellhound shot past Jim and into the fray. Eddie leveled his shotgun and fired.

O O O

Crannock Castle, the West Country

ENGLISH CIVIL WAR

BOOOOOOM!

The guns on the wall of Crannock Castle roared, defying the rabble of Roundheads surrounding the moldering old fortress. At the parapet stood Elaine, hair unbound and blowing free in the wind and the smoke. The torchlight made her long blonde hair shine like a heaven-flowing river of gold, and her eyes glittered.

James shifted uneasily, eyeing the flints on both his pistols. The rain had stopped, but his powder was still wet and useless.

He lay concealed on a wooded hill within earshot of the castle's gate and the crowd in front of it. The Roundheads had slack defenses, maybe indicating that they knew the fate of Matthew Taylor's men. That, the darkness, and the careful slitting of a few throats had let James slip this close.

"Stand aside, girl!" yelled Sir John Horsham. He sat astride a big horse, clad in neck cloth and mail, the rolls of merchant's fat around his neck no doubt making it hard to breathe. He was armed like a warrior, at least, with a brace of pistols and a basket-hilted broadsword hanging from his sash. Around him were his senior aides and other leaders of the Parliamentarian force besieging the castle. They all looked like burghers and aldermen, but James knew they were soldiers to be feared. More so, given the armed masses of buff-coated men at their backs. "Let us speak with the master of this place!"

Elaine laughed, and James fell in love all over again. Her laughter was fierce and free. It was the way a hawk might laugh, mocking pursuers and defying all the world to catch it or show it cause. James could be free with a laugh like that, alone together and free together, forever. He sighed.

Where was the old man? James wondered.

"Why, Sir John!" Elaine called to the Parliamentarian leader. "'Tis good of you to come all this long road in person, but I fear that we are already well supplied with Cambridge wool! But if you wish to give any of your wares as gifts to your king, leave them at the gate, and I shall see that His Majesty receives them!"

The pork-faced burghers harrumphed and snorted.

"You are encircled!" Sir John waved at the banks of glaring guns rolling into place in a circle around Crannock in the surrounding wooded hills, the ranks of cavalrymen ready to mount, and the musketeers. "Is that all you have to say?"

Elaine rotated in the breeze, looking at the armies about her ancestral manse and her own pitifully small cluster of men, bunched in their green livery all along the castle's battlements like so much moss. When she had taken it all in, she turned back to her attacker.

Surrender, James willed her. *Surrender or stall.* If they blasted her off the wall with cannons, there was nothing he could do. If they settled in for a siege or took her prisoner, he might still stand a chance.

"I do have other things to say to you, Sir John!" Elaine Canning admitted. "But I would not wish to scorch the ears of your delicate lady companions, and I do not know if you own a goat!"

Her own men laughed uproariously, though they stayed hunkered down behind the stone walls. The East Anglians and Kentishmen standing at the gate looked considerably less amused.

"Your father!" Sir John snapped. From his vantage point, James saw blue veins standing out in the increasingly ruddy flesh of the man's face. "I will speak with your father!"

"Will you?" Elaine called. "I have not spoken with him for days! Or rather, he has not spoken to me."

Sir John faltered. The feeling of dread in the pit of James's stomach matched the expression on Sir John's face. "Where is he, witch?"

Elaine disappeared behind one of the wall's crenels. The men at the gate shifted uneasily in their saddles for a moment, but then she reappeared, stepping lightly into the crenel between the merlons.

"Here he is!" she cried, and held something up.

It was her father's severed head.

The Roundheads backed their horses, gasping and cursing. A tall, bony Parliamentarian with stringy black hair leaned over and vomited on the ground.

Sir John shook his fist at his enemy on the wall. "As you brew, hag, so shall you drink!"

"Oh, Sir John!" she snapped back. "That is surely true of all of us. It was true, for instance, of my father!" She leaned back to get maximum leverage, then hurled her father's head at her foes.

The Roundheads saw the macabre missile coming and didn't wait for it. Wheeling, they bolted back for their lines.

The head of the former lord of Crannock Castle thudded off the green grass just behind the hooves of the last of their horses and rolled, coming to a stop face up and looking across the battlefield-to-be at James.

"God's wounds," James muttered. "This takes a dark turn."

O O O

The Ruins of Ainok and the Gate of Hell

THE END OF THE AGE OF PISCES

Two of Mab's Rangers bounded forward, flashing in and out of their animal forms and barreling for Jim. Looking at the shimmering ocelot-puck-goose and hippopotamus-brownie-cobra coming his way, Jim felt tired.

It was almost over now, he told himself. Soon he would be with her.

Still, he was happy when Eddie blasted one of the Rangers sideways with his shotgun. The squirming hippo splashed loudly into the oily waters of the lake and vanished.

Jim grabbed the goose around the neck. When it honked, he squeezed, cutting off the protest. The goose slithered into an ocelot, and he punched it in the face with the basket hilt of Sir John Horsham's sword, battering it silly. He threw the hapless Ranger aside, into the deadly waters.

There were too many. Jim heard guns going off at his shoulder, but the bullets wouldn't inflict much harm on the fairy warriors or the Wild Things. Grenades or plastic explosives would have come in handy, but if the band had any left, they were in the crumpled wreckage of Eddie's old Dodge van back in Kansas City. A good firebolt from Adrian Pew would've been handy too.

Only Adrian had died at the Crossroads, incinerated by the oldest enemy of order itself.

Rangers swarmed over Jim. He was buffeted back and forth, but when he saw three of the fairies piling onto Twitch, he kicked his way through the mass of Mab's children and grabbed his drummer by the shoulders.

The fairy felt like paper under his touch, and it looked up at him with liquid eyes.

"Adrian," Twitch said.

Jim batted away a spider monkey and tried to think of something to say. He had nothing, and then a ram knocked him sideways and off balance. Brass hooves flashed over his head from something that looked like a wolf but had mandibles and antennae like an ant.

Bang!

Another gun fired.

Jim felt his mind slip. He grabbed for it but missed, and then it was gone.

The hooves above him melted away like July snow. A Valkyrie crashed over his field of vision, black wings spread wide, her mount's body stretching into a long leap, and fire pouring from her hands. A screech like the world was splitting apart pounded through Jim's head like a sonic nail. He thought he might be screaming, though he couldn't be sure.

A dark creature in his hands spat blood at him and hissed, showing long fangs. Jim stabbed it—

And then something fast and green hit him, knocking him down. He raised his sword, but the green bolt kicked it aside with hard hooves. His assailant loomed over him, tall and black with a twisted, demonic face and skinny arms. It pointed a rod at him, a scepter of fire and death.

Jim pushed off the ground with his ankles. His body pivoted upward on his ground-rooted shoulders, and he kicked the demon in the back of its head. It stumbled forward and off of Jim.

Jim rolled to his feet, looking for his sword.

The demon kicked it further away.

The screeching sound shredded Jim's eardrums. The spitting black thing sank teeth into Jim's hip. Somewhere, something called him. This all seemed wrong. Something bad was happening, something Jim couldn't quite understand, though he tried to force his mind to it.

He rammed his shoulder into the wand-wielding demon, knocking it back. As it fell, it kneed him in the face and he tumbled away.

He groped for the sword but couldn't find it. The biting thing scratched at his head and neck, and he grabbed its neck with his off hand.

Wand-demon kicked Jim in the gut. The force of the blow lifted him off the ground an inch, and he flipped over onto his back, spread-eagled. Wand-demon rose to its full towering height, bellowing and pointing the wand at Jim. Above the demon, the sky swirled in yellow and green streaks that coruscated and shifted in sync with the scratching, whistling sounds in his head.

Jim's outstretched hand found the hilt of his sword. He snatched it, pointing it up at Wand-demon—

And a wave of cool air snapped across him.

For a moment he thought he was in the hills of the West Country. Elaine ran before him, holding up her long skirts the color of the cool grass over which she ran. He grabbed her arm, pulling her to himself.

"Stop!" Eddie shouted.

There was no Wand-demon and no Elaine; there was only Eddie Marlowe, cursed family man, ex-Marine, and mediocre guitar player. Eddie stood over Jim and leaned forward, pointing his shotgun down.

"I don't want to have to shoot you, Jim!" Eddie yelled. "But I will if I have to! Let Twitch go!"

Jim looked down at himself. He held his sword in his right hand, but the fingers of his left were clenched tight around Twitch's neck, squeezing the fairy's throat so hard that its choke was silent and breathless. Twitch scrabbled at Jim's arm with limp, weak hands, and its eyes bugged out.

Jim released his drummer.

"Sorry." He climbed to his knees.

"Drop the sword!" Eddie shouted.

"I'm fine," Jim told him.

"What?" Eddie was still bellowing.

Earplugs. The madness that had taken Jim hadn't touched Eddie because he was wearing his earplugs.

Qayna. Crow Jane, they had called her in the trenches of the Great War, where death and madness rode in her wake. The bullets of her cursed gun could kill immortals, and the report when she fired tortured the minds of everyone in earshot.

He dropped his sword and raised his hands in surrender.

"You sure know how to show a girl a good time," Twitch muttered. It stood, but it didn't straighten its back out of a crooked hunch.

"I didn't mean it," Jim said.

"It's okay. I was pretty sure you were Buzzard Betsy."

"What's that?"

The fairy shook its head. "Does it matter?"

Clopping hooves cut the conversation short as Qayna returned. Her big black horse dripped blood from its sharp teeth.

Jim looked beyond the rider. A pair of Hellhounds wrestled with a chain-belted ogress, a heavy thing with talons and a lipless mouth. The Infernal toad-beast tore into a knot of fairy Rangers. The Legate's golems, burnt black and missing parts but still moving, harried Baraqyel and kept him at bay. It looked like a stalemate, though a fragile and thrashing one.

Another heavy *boom!* rang out, this one accompanied by a faint trembling of the earth under Jim's feet, reminding him that the Baobab was coming.

"You're here for the Council," Qayna said. It wasn't a question.

Twitch shuffled sideways, away from the mounted woman. Eddie spun to deliver a roundhouse kick that knocked a baboon off Mike's back. The baboon hit the ground in the shape of a fat spider and scuttled away up the road. Eddie dragged Mike to his feet.

"*Mierda.*"

"Yeah, enchilada to you too." Eddie scooped Mike's dropped pistol off the ground and dragged him back towards the open gate.

More chaos-formed, mutilated, twisted things spewed forth from the gate; others trickled down the hill. With a blast from his shotgun, Eddie knocked back something with three legs and an open mouth facing downward at the mud.

"Which ones are on our side?" Mike yelled, his voice hard to hear in the din.

"When in doubt," Eddie hollered back—*boom!* His shotgun shredded two buzzing Zvuvim into black paper.

"Yes," Jim admitted to Qayna. "I'm here for the Council. And you?"

"This is the Liminal Year," she said. "All things are possible."

"The cosmos shifts gears," he agreed.

"Besides." Qayna looked around her, keeping her seat easily as her horse kicked away a writhing knot of serpents. "When there's only one game in town … where else you gonna go?"

Jim's laugh sounded harsh to his own ears.

Baraqyel slammed his immense spear through three of the golems in a single blow. The spear sank several feet into rock, pinning them. As the Legate scampered forward, raising his hands in some arcane gesture, Baraqyel grabbed the fourth golem—the headless one—by its legs and picked it up off the ground. He swung the golem like a club.

The Legate danced back, knocked off-balance, and Baraqyel hurled the golem over its master's head and into the lake.

"Go!" Baraqyel called to Jim, taking a step back from the advancing mass and letting a Hellhound rush past him to do some of the heavy lifting for a moment. "Your father is expecting you!"

"He is, is he?" Jim couldn't help curling his lips into a tight sneer.

Eddie dragged Mike. The big bass player looked shocked and disoriented. Qayna offered a hand to Twitch and, after a moment's hesitation, the drummer took it. Qayna pulled the fairy onto the front of her saddle and urged her horse forward, past a stream of slavering troll-creatures.

The iron gates loomed huge around Jim as he passed through. Within, two faceless giants stood, each grasping a ringed grip with both hands.

Jim turned to take one last look at the winking star whose arrival signaled the Liminal Year, and at Baraqyel and the faithful hordes of Hell, battling the armies of the Mirror Queendom, the Legate of Heaven, and the rebel minions of Belial. The lake's waters rippled, and a gray arm—a golem's arm—surged from the depths. It clawed at the dark air twice, fingers closing over nothing, and then fell beneath the surface again.

Was *dragged* beneath.

Qayna trotted in through the gates and past him, followed by Mike and Eddie.

The Baobab loomed out of the mist, a sudden skyscraper of charging tree.

"The door, Baraqyel!" Jim snapped, but the Fallen didn't turn his head.

It was a hell of a time to show pique. Jim shouted a word of command in Infernal, and the blank-faced giants threw their bodies into the effort. With an immense grating sound and a final *BOOM*, they slammed the gate shut.

CHAPTER TWO

The City of Ainok

THE END OF THE AGE OF GEMINI

I did not intend this."

Jacob bar Azazel looked up at his father. Jacob was as small as any of the children of men, wiry and strong but little. He was just a boy, though his father was a titan and a Prince. His father was Azazel, first of the Fallen. Though with sorcerous operations Azazel had reformed his body, he had kept his original Heaven-given stature. He had been a Bearer of the Word, and he still towered over his son, his goatlike legs and bat wings casting a shadow that covered the entire platform at the top of Ainok's central Tower.

Jacob didn't want goat legs or bat wings or a Princely title. He wanted to be with his father. He had never known his mother, and the fact that he was his father's son isolated him from those around him. He could not be proper friends with his father's rivals or his subjects or his slaves. He and his father were alone, but at least they were alone together.

Azazel, first of the Princes of Ainok, looked out over his City of the Free, and his son turned and followed his gaze.

The city was sluiced by its great canals. They brought bright, clean water over sparkling stones from the Rivers of Eden in an immense spiral that touched the very middle of Ainok. The water made a single twist around the Grand Plaza in the city's center and then spun back out again, a second spiral within the first that carried the city's filth out and away to the foul, swampy lake to its south. From the ground, the canals appeared to be an impenetrable maze of long, curving main branches and shorter tributaries, some of clean water and some inexplicably foul. From above, the pattern of running water looked like a gigantic flower.

The plain was almost perfectly flat. Enchantment made the water flow.

The canals crossed broad plazas and ran along wide boulevards. Every building in Ainok was squarely framed of dark wood and white stone, and everything sparkled. Ordinarily, that sparkle would have been complemented by the incessant bustle of a people about its business. The boulevards were wide to accommodate wagons and caravans, and the plazas left plenty of space for merchants' booths. Now, as the first burning stink of the smoky trails of the falling Bearers of the Sword reached Jacob's nostrils, the Free People fled. They jammed the city's gates and streets, trampling each other and staining the streets red with their blood and the blood of their animals.

The Fallen ran too, trampling the smaller folk under hoof and claw in their flight.

"They came in tents at first," Azazel continued. "They had heard of my rebellion, and though I raised no flag, they came to me anyway. *I* was their flag. Some of them wanted to be powerful. All of them wanted to be free." He turned and looked at his son, and his eyes were warm. "Everyone wants to be free. Not everyone understands the price."

"What's the price, Papa?" Jacob asked. The top of the Tower felt intimate, warm, and safe even though the wrath of Heaven fell from the skies all around them and Azazel's people massacred itself in the streets below. Everything but the platform was remote and unreal, not urgent. His father would protect him.

Azazel turned again and looked down at the city. "When you are free," he rumbled, his voice like a lion's warning growl, "you must bear all the consequences of your actions alone."

Jacob considered this. "What do you mean?"

His father sighed. "I mean that the city of tents became unlivable. We walked in our own excrement. We ate and breathed flies, and our own flesh hosted their eggs. I could not sleep for the sounds of rutting and murder about me at all times."

"Did you stay because of me?"

Azazel laughed and knelt. Standing at his father's knee and under his wings was as good as being inside a building. Jacob grinned as his father gently mussed his hair. "I would have," the Prince of the Free agreed, "but you did not exist then. I had not even met your mother."

Jacob didn't know his mother. He nodded, eager to hear the story though he didn't understand it.

"I built this city." Azazel stood again, his heavy hooves clicking loudly on the white flagstones that paved the Tower's platform. He stretched an enormous arm to point as he spoke. "I barred access to this plain while I worked, and I began by flooding it to clean it of the filth that was here. I dug the canals myself. I plowed the guiding lines into the ground, and I laid the incantations by my own hand. I marked out the Grand Plaza and the Palace, but the first building I raised was this Tower, and here I finally planted my banner. And then I opened the roads again."

"And they came, Papa."

Azazel nodded solemnly. "They came. They gathered in the Plaza and heard my rules, and they agreed to them. We would be rebels, but we would rebel together, and our burdens would be shared. I did this, you understand, for myself."

"And also it made other people happy."

Azazel shrugged. "Yes."

"And now?"

Azazel looked to the horizon. Bearers of the Sword strode across fruited fields, igniting them with their fiery white touch. Jacob trembled to look at the vengeful angels, faces entirely hidden behind platelike visors and tree-sized swords dripping liquid fire on the ground, but his father looked calm. Resolved.

"Now," Azazel said slowly, "I wonder if I have taken full enough account of what the consequences and the burdens really are."

The first of the Bearers of the Sword reached the wall. It raised its enormous weapon overhead and swung it down like an ax. Masonry exploded on contact with the sword, blasting out over the fleeing crowds and leaving bloody furrows behind.

Azazel turned suddenly, looking down. He guffawed, a sound like an earthquake's groan but joyous. Jacob looked at the Grand Plaza but didn't see what his father was laughing at. Then Azazel snatched his son, held him close to his chest, and vaulted into the air.

The world flashed about them, but Jacob didn't close his eyes. His heart thrilled to be this close to his father. He was an only son, but his father had many women and many courtiers and rivals and allies on Ainok's Council, so he had little time, generally, for Jacob. He wondered if their separation made his father feel lonely too. The height and speed of the movement didn't frighten Jacob, and he tightened his arms against his father's enormous body and enjoyed the trembling, vibrating feeling of flight.

They alighted with birdlike grace, and Azazel set his son down. A woman stood there—a woman to Jacob's scale rather than Azazel's. She had long black hair, skin as brown as a nut, and anxiety written on her face as plainly as the blue tattoos that covered and identified her. She held a knife in her hand. There was something otherworldly or shifty about her; she continually squinted left or right, as if seeing phantoms invisible to others.

She was Qayna, the Marked Woman. She was a frequent visitor at Ainok; she had some history with his father, and Jacob didn't understand quite what it was. But he knew that

Qayna had done something Heaven didn't like, and as a result she had been cursed to wander the earth forever.

He wasn't sure if that made her like his father, or his opposite.

She looked at Jacob, and he looked back.

"You must take Jacob and flee."

"The Swordbearers are here!" Qayna said. She waved her knife in a big circle, as if to show that they were surrounded.

Azazel smiled gently, but Jacob thought his father was keeping strong emotions bottled up. Jacob had a feeling, and he couldn't quite tell himself why, that his forced departure was another of his father's ... consequences. Burdens. "Must I repeat myself? I took you in when you had no place else to go, Qayna. Will you not repay the favor?"

Qayna took Jacob's hand, and then a whirlwind of action exploded around them. Jacob watched with feelings that were half-sickness and half-detachment as his father fended off a rough challenge from the brutish, pig-headed Semyaz, mocking and then leaving his rival buried in rubble. And then Jacob and Qayna were running past a snake-headed giant and into the glittering city.

She dragged him along by main force. A Bearer of the Sword nearly killed him when Qayna ran down the wrong alley. Jacob didn't cry. He wondered what would happen if the big flaming sword that reduced stone buildings to smoking rubble hit the Marked Woman. Would it kill her, or would her curse protect her?

And what if the sword killed Jacob? It surely would if it hit him. What would be the cause of that consequence? Whose choices would have been the cause of Jacob's death?

Ainok was the only home Jacob had ever known, and he watched it blasted, smashed, and burned around him as they ran. He was a little surprised when the tough, dense hardwoods burned, but he was shocked to see stone itself burst into flame. The Free ran without coordination, and they died alone, ten thousand horrible, mangled deaths, as Jacob and his bodyguard rushed unnoticed among them. Then, as the Marked Woman dragged him along a canal, its murky, waste-bearing waters now slightly darker with the blood that sluiced into it from the city streets, he saw his father again.

Azazel stood on the other side of the canal. Jacob had run across most of Ainok only to be within yards of the father he'd left. The Prince of the Free was now surrounded by multiple Bearers of the Sword, along with a single Bearer of the Word.

Jacob didn't know any of the agents of Heaven personally because they never came to the Free City. They had never come, anyway, until today. But this figure was the height of his father and drifted slightly off the ground, lifted by six wings that rarely actually moved. It was like he floated, and occasionally fluttered his wings to give the floating direction, which was very different from the muscular, animal flight of Jacob's father. The Bearer of the Word burned white.

This was how Jacob's father had looked before he had chosen to look otherwise. Of course, Jacob had never seen him like that.

"Have you come to spout more defiance?" the Wordbearer demanded. Jacob tried to stop, though he had no way to intervene and no hope of standing against Heaven's armies. It didn't matter; Qayna dragged him along, all his resistance amounting to nothing.

"What defiance?" Even his father's surrender looked proud and noble. "I am defeated, and I have come for punishment. Leave the others be. They harm no one. They only wish to be free."

Was he laying down his freedom for his son only? Jacob wondered. Or did Azazel really feel the benevolence towards his subjects as he claimed?

Qayna yanked Jacob's arm and dragged him on, but he kept watching as she ran.

"For you, there is no punishment."

"No?" Jacob thought his father looked amused. The Swordbearers closed in around him.

"Punishment is for violations of the law. What you did was so unthinkable, it was against no law. It was inconceivable until you did it."

Azazel laughed. "If I have broken no law, what are you doing here? If I have broken no law, how can there be a Writ for the Bearers of the Sword to execute? Or is Heaven now breaking its own laws?"

One of the Bearers of the Sword put away his weapon with a deep, shuddering rasp. From some unimaginable place on his person, he produced a long, silver-blue, shimmering length of chain.

"Your choice—your action—is to be erased." The Bearer of the Word smiled. The expression chilled Jacob to his bones. "Undone. Blotted out. This is the Writ that has issued. This is what the Bearers of the Sword have come to do."

"Heaven eliminates its rivals." Azazel laughed. "And then it tries again."

Qayna shuddered to a halt, and Jacob bounced off her hip. He didn't see why she had stopped; he couldn't take his eyes off his father. The Bearers of the Sword and the Word wrapped chains around Azazel, Prince of the Free. Jacob felt tears sting his eyes.

"You are not Heaven's rival," the Bearer of the Word sneered when the chains were in place.

Jacob was dimly aware that Qayna was trading words with bearded, armed, and armored men beside the canal. He couldn't see them through his tears, and he couldn't focus hard enough to make out their words.

"No?" Azazel thundered. He drew himself up to his full height. Even with glittering chains pinning his wings to his shoulders, he looked mighty, fearsome, and dangerous. The Bearer of the Word shriveled slightly and shrank back under the assault of Azazel's glaring eyes. "Then what am I?"

Qayna dove into the water, dragging Jacob with her.

He struggled. He didn't try to get away from her, but without thinking about it, he reached to grab his father as he fell and drag Azazel with them. Of course he missed. He was so far from his father it might as well have been leagues, and he kicked in rage as the cold, filthy waters swallowed him.

He continued kicking, angry and uncomprehending, as he felt the walls of Ainok pass over his head. He kicked as thick river bottom weeds wrapped around him and Qayna and she cut them away to carry them both on. And as cold needles stabbed deep into his brain and robbed Jacob bar Azazel of consciousness, he kicked one final time.

In that last moment, looking up through the silt- and blood-laden water at a shimmering curtain of daylight, he would have sworn he saw a figure looking down at him. A figure whose name he didn't know, but whom he recognized as one of the Princes of Ainok—a shapeless, tentacled figure with a snapping beak.

Then, blackness.

O O O

"Do I have a choice?"

Jacob opened his eyes, and the monstrous figure was gone. He saw fire through water.

At first, he thought in his disorientation that he was looking down into a bowl of water and that beneath the gently-rippling concentric rings on the bowl's surface, someone had placed diamonds full of fire. He had seen more than enough sorcery at his father's court not to find that astonishing.

But then he realized that he wasn't hanging facedown. He was faceup. And that realization did astonish him.

Because it meant that he was still lying beneath water. Not Ainok's canal any longer, but a large font or bowl. The rings he saw were above him, not below, and the brilliantly burning gems were outside the water.

He wasn't breathing, but the needle in his brain was gone.

"Yes," said a second voice, and Jacob realized that the first voice he'd heard belonged to his father. The second was deeper, which barely seemed possible. "You have always had choices."

Jacob tried to inhale but couldn't. His lungs wouldn't move. He tried to stretch forth his hand and touch the surface of the pool, but he couldn't do that, either.

Am I dead? he wondered.

"But doesn't that make a mockery of everything you've just told me?"

A long silence.

Jacob focused on his body, trying to reassure himself that he hadn't lost sensation. It was hard to tell without being able to move. He didn't feel warm, but he wasn't cold either. His eyelids seemed to be the only thing he could move, and all they could do was slowly blink open and shut.

He heard Azazel speak again. "'A choice between two opposites,' you said. 'Light and dark, good and evil, and the inevitability of cause and effect,' you said."

More silence. Jacob strained his concentration, trying to will his muscles to push his legs beneath himself so he could stand. He had no idea what he'd see if he succeeded, but in the end, it didn't matter. His limbs refused to obey his command. More sorcery.

"A house is built in stages. A plan unfolds one step at a time."

Jacob wondered who his father was talking to. It wasn't a voice he recognized, and his father's words had an uncharacteristic sound to them. They were … restrained. Calm. Meek? He didn't think that could possibly be the right word, but he didn't have another. His father addressed someone who was not his subject and who was maybe, just maybe, his superior.

"So I just accept that this is another stage of the gradually self-revealing plan?"

"The plan is not self-revealing."

"No?"

"*I* reveal it."

"I stand corrected. How long will the revelation take?"

"Until the end of time."

This time it was his father's turn to be silent. After long moments, he asked, "So … forever?"

There was no answer.

"What is the alternative for me, then?" Azazel continued. "Life and death, corruption and incorruption, happiness and misery … if I do not accept this burden, what horrible end awaits me?"

"There is a true exile."

"You say that as if it were a curse. But I chose as I did thinking that I *was* choosing exile in truth. I didn't expect this audience. I certainly didn't seek it."

"There are consequences for the child too."

Another long silence followed, and then a visible form appeared above Jacob, blocking out some of the burning lights. Jacob couldn't make out details on the silhouetted shape, but when it suddenly stretched enormous, batlike wings and revealed a human-shaped head and shoulders, he knew it was his father.

A small disturbance dimpled the surface of the water. Then another.

Then Azazel, First Prince of Ainok, knelt. In the changed light resulting from his movement, his son saw his face and saw that his cheeks glistened.

More disturbance of the surface above.

Tears, Jacob realized. His father wept.

"You force my hand."

"No." The answer was immediate but gentle. "There is compassion for you too."

"Only after you break my spirit with punishment."

"No punishment. Cause and effect. Consequences."

"The difference eludes me." Another shadow crossed the surface of the water, wavering, and Jacob realized that it was his father's hand, stretched forth and hovering just above the water. He longed to reach up and take his father's hand, but he couldn't.

"I don't choose the consequences. They are necessary. In the end, they may be for the good."

Azazel sprang to his feet, the near-clarity of his face again fading into remote shadow. "That is the essence of it. I deny that I have any choice in this matter, but I accept what is forced upon me. I will bear this burden."

"It will be a long and hard road."

"I will do it for my son."

A pause.

"Now he is my son too."

The words didn't sound like a welcome, though. They sounded like a sentence.

Chapter Three

Palestine

THE WANING YEARS OF THE AGE OF ARIES

Jacob bar Abbas smiled and said nothing. He knew it would make the Roman mad. Being angry made people stupid. So did being greedy and eager. And he wanted the Roman to be stupid.

"When does the Liminal Year begin? Is it this equinox?"

The Roman was a paunchy man, prematurely bald, with a vicious sneer in the proud hook of his nose. He crouched in the dungeon before Jacob, illuminated by a single torch in a bracket set into the wall, looking into his chained prisoner's eyes for any sign of recognition or surrender.

Behind him stood his two kilt-clad, deaf-mute assistants. They were tall, as tall as Jacob, though where he was as pale as ivory even after years in this dusty desert crossroads, they were as black as black could be. Abyssinians, he guessed from their faces. He was broader in the shoulders than they were, but they were fat and muscled, and Jacob's frame had wasted away in the holding cell. The Roman wouldn't use his own men for this interrogation—he wouldn't want them to learn the secrets he was after. So instead, he used these slaves. He'd probably kill them when he was finished. He'd kill all three of them.

That might be interesting.

But really, it was better that Jacob just escape before it came to that. Also, it was better that he not give anything away. He had no way of knowing whom the Roman might serve. He also had no way of knowing where his sorcerer friend had gone. Why hadn't Ishbaal rescued him yet? Was there another wizard at work here?

He laughed. He was perfectly capable of matching the Roman's cosmopolitan Latin, but he deliberately spoke in rough, tribal tones. "You tell me, Roman. You seem to know much."

In the interrogation's pause, the chanting of the crowd outside became louder. "Bar Abbas, bar Abbas, bar Abbas!" they rumbled. Jacob repressed a grin. The fact that the window through which the sound came was fifteen feet off the ground was not a problem. The fact that the window was barred and Jacob was chained to the wall with iron links was a real obstacle.

The Roman stood, chewing his lip. He moved away and gestured to one of the Abyssinians. The big man stepped in close to Jacob and knotted his fingers in Jacob's long black hair. The Roman took a short, leisurely stroll once about the vaulted cell while the African pounded Jacob repeatedly in the mouth.

Jacob fought to keep his grin plastered on his face. The blows smarted.

When the Roman returned, the Abyssinian tossed Jacob to the ground and stepped back.

"The soldiers who cornered you in the Golden Gate reported that you were a Scythian. You're no Scythian."

"I smell too nice?" Jacob grinned. The taste of his own blood filled his mouth.

"You smell too bad." The Roman frowned. "You positively stink."

"So bathe me."

"I know that the Council meets at the opening of the Liminal Year. *Always*. And also at the close."

"Yeah? What Council?"

"On Earth as it is in Heaven. When the sky shifts, we enter the Age of the Fish—a new heaven and a new earth."

Jacob scratched himself and grunted.

"We approach the Liminal Year," the Roman continued. "Hence, the wonders in the sky. The monsters on Earth and spewing up from the deep. Two-headed babies, fish that walk upon the land, new stars … all mark the impending time of great change. And in the Liminal Year, during the transition, all bonds are loosened, all pacts are void, all things are possible. The Council sits to elect a new First Prince, a new Accuser."

"Council?" Jacob yawned. "Prince? I thought you were a prefect or a governor or something."

The Roman laughed. "And you, Jacob *bar Abbas*, are clearly no Scythian."

"I never said I was."

"Thank you for dropping the bad accent."

"What accent do you think I should have?"

The Roman shot a quick sidelong glance at one of his Abyssinians and narrowed his eyelids. "A much … *older* accent."

Jacob looked from one Abyssinian to the other, slowly examining them. "I assume you've taken these men's tongues."

The Roman nodded. "Of course."

"How certain are you of their deafness? Can they read lips? Can they read and write?"

"What are you suggesting?"

"I'm suggesting that if I had anything interesting to discuss with you, I certainly wouldn't want to risk it becoming public."

The Roman looked smug. "I trust these men."

Jacob leaned forward slowly, eyeing the two slaves skeptically. "Are you even sure they're the men you think they are?"

The Roman looked startled. "Do you mean … sorcery?"

"What else are we talking about?"

The Roman leaned close. So close he was within reach, though the Abyssinians watched like vultures. "Do not toy with me, Jacob bar Abbas." His breath was heavy with cumin and fish sauce. "I mean to have power."

"So do I, Pilate," Jacob lied.

"Bar Abbas, bar Abbas!" the crowd rumbled.

The Roman stood. "Leave us!" He flung his arms at the door in a gesture of command.

The Abyssinians ducked subserviently and padded out.

Standing at the door behind them, Pontius Pilate muttered an incantation. *Sumerian*, Jacob thought, *grammatically rough but serviceable.* So there *was* another sorcerer in the mix. Jacob's mental wheels ground a little more, and he felt something like hope.

"A powerful magician like you," he said. "I can't imagine what you need me for."

"I don't need you to lock a door, Jacob *bar Azazel*." Pontius Pilate paced closer but still well out of Jacob's reach. "I need you to get me into the Council meeting, which none may attend but by right or by invitation."

Jacob nodded slowly. "You're right, I am bar Azazel."

"Lucifer's son, heir to the Morning Throne. In exile among the lowly mortals of this world. A falling out with your illustrious father?"

"I'm here by choice." Jacob watched the Roman carefully and ignored the upwelling emotions within him. It was true, he was something of an exile. After Jacob's death and return, his father had never looked at him the same way again. Unable to explain or understand, and unwilling to tell his father what he had seen beneath the water in the pool of his own death, Jacob had instead taken to wandering. "I can go back any time I want to. I just save it for important occasions."

"Good. That's just what I need. A short trip home with a new friend—me—is clearly an important occasion."

"I can't help you."

Pilate screwed his face into a suspicious fist. "I'm glad you drop the pretenses. Now, if you can let down your maidenly reluctance, perhaps we can get to business."

Jacob chuckled and leaned back. He rested his shoulders against the base of the cell wall, his sandaled feet sprawling out on the floor. "I lost my shyness centuries ago, Roman. The problem is that it isn't possible."

The Roman arched an eyebrow. "If that's really true, then I have no use for you and will have you executed."

"And piss off the mob?"

Pilate snorted. "I am a Roman and a soldier."

"Exactly."

Pilate put his hand on the dagger belted at his waist. "The only thing keeping you alive at this moment is the fact that I don't believe you, bar Azazel. I suggest you choose your next words very carefully. A retraction and offer to do what I want *will* suffice. An alternative suggestion *might*. Anything else signs your own death sentence."

Jacob sighed. "Here's how it is: When were you born?"

The Roman furrowed his brow. "Why do you care?"

Paranoid bastard. "I don't. But I assume you're less than a century old."

"Go on." Pilate's voice was cold, but held a note of curiosity.

"You'd have to be thousands of years old to be admitted. Not as a policy. As a matter of simple physical fact."

"I'm in no mood for riddles," the Roman snarled, but the snarl was halfhearted, and the narrowing of his eyes suggested that a riddle might be exactly what he was in the mood for.

"How long have you been in Judea, Pilate?"

"I'm tired of the questions, darkling. Time for answers."

Jacob nodded and sighed, holding up his hands in surrender. Pilate shuffled half a step closer. Jacob explained, "The Jews have an old story in their book of Judges. The Gileadites had defeated the Ephraimites and were guarding a ford on the river. They wanted to make sure none of the Ephraimites got through. 'When those Ephraimites which were escaped said, Let me go over; that the men of Gilead said unto him, Art thou an Ephraimite? If he said, Nay; Then said they unto him, Say now *Shibboleth*: and he said *Sibboleth*: for he could not frame to pronounce it right. Then they took him, and slew him at the passages of Jordan.'"

Pilate cocked his head and released his grip on his dagger. "A password."

"Exactly."

"I can say *Shibboleth*, bar Azazel."

"True. But you don't speak Infernal."

"You can teach me."

"You're not capable of learning."

The Roman put his hand on the dagger again. "Are you insulting me?" He stepped another half step closer.

Jacob shook his head. "More ancient stories. Really, you're never going to get anywhere unless you learn the true history of the world."

"So tell me," Pilate growled.

Jacob sighed. He carefully kept his eyes fixed on a point on the floor between his knees. "A long time ago, a group of people wanted to get to Heaven. Without permission, you understand? They wanted to force their way in, get a heavenly name. I'm still not sure their plan made any sense, but what they did was build the world's tallest tower. Ever."

Pilate snorted, but his eyes flashed. "Jewish nonsense."

Jacob shook his head. "I was there. It might have been nonsense, but it wasn't Jewish. It was long before the world saw its first Jew or even its first Hebrew. I don't know whether they would have succeeded; Heaven didn't let them finish anyway. It shattered the tower, and it cursed the entire race with the Confusion of the Tongues."

"Idiotic. This is an old fable. You're telling me that after this ... this *construction project gone wrong*, mankind spoke separate languages."

"That's one thing that happened," Jacob agreed. "Another thing that happened is that they forgot the original languages. Not only forgot them, but their descendants born into the Confusion forever after lost the ability to speak them, remember them, or even hear them clearly."

"Original languages?"

"Adamic was the original human tongue," Jacob said. "Angelic and Infernal are closely related."

The Roman hesitated, then rocked back a step. "I don't believe it."

"If I told you the password a thousand times," Jacob shrugged, "you wouldn't be able to remember it."

"Liar." But the Roman looked convinced.

"Ten thousand times. You probably wouldn't even *hear* it."

Pontius Pilate bared straight white teeth. "Try me."

"You're an idiot." Jacob said it in Infernal.

A flicker passed over Pilate's face. "I said try me," he repeated himself. "Say the password."

Jacob laughed. "I did."

Pilate frowned and stared. "Liar."

"I'll do it again." Jacob shifted to Infernal. "You're an idiot. You're a flyblown, goat-humping moron."

The Roman shook his head. "You're just moving your lips silently."

Jacob ran his fingers through his hair. "No, really, I'm not. This is the problem, you see. I tell you the password, and you can't even hear it. You never will, no matter how often I say it or how loud."

"Shout."

Jacob looked at the door. "Really?"

Pilate nodded. He muttered more Sumerian, gesturing over his own face. Then he stepped closer, leaned forward, and cupped one hand around his ear. "Shout it as loud as you can."

"Okay." Jacob cleared his throat. He hollered, again in Infernal, "You really are just too damn stupid to live!"

The word *damn* in Infernal ruffled the hair around Pilate's ears, and the Roman's eyes widened in surprise. As his mouth split into a grin and he started to say something, Jacob kicked him as hard as he could in the crotch.

Pilate rose into the air, his eyes growing even wider. His arms flapped wide like wings, and as he came down, Jacob caught him with both hands, one around Pilate's throat and the other gripping the Roman by his fighting wrist.

"Mrump—" Jacob choked the Roman's words into silence, then twisted and slammed his enemy to the floor. Before the sorcerer could do anything but arch his back in pain, Jacob was on top of him, chains clanking heavily as he drew the other man's dagger and pressed it against his throat.

Jacob's toes *hurt*.

"I know," Jacob hissed savagely into Pilate's ear, ignoring the throbbing in his feet. He didn't have any attention to spare for the door; he just had to act fast and hope for the best. He pushed the dagger hard enough to draw blood from under the Roman's jaw. "This wasn't how you expected things to go. But that's a toga for you—no protection where you need it."

Pilate's eyes bugged out of his face. Hungry, battered, and anxious for his freedom as he was, Jacob still had to laugh.

He shook his chained wrist, knocking heavy links against the Roman's face. "I, on the other hand, feel that the night is finally headed in the right direction. The next thing that will happen is that you're going to use one of your spells to unlock me."

Pilate arched his thin eyebrows skeptically. Jim relaxed his grip just a hair, and the Roman snorted.

"Here's the thing," Jacob continued. "I understand Sumerian, believe it or not, because I was once a camel driver in Sumer, and I heard you cast your spell locking the door. So I know you can do it, and I know more or less what the spell will sound like. So you're going to cast the spell I ask— *exactly that spell*, and nothing else—or I'll simply kill you."

"And then?" the Roman croaked, hard put to squeeze air through Jacob's grip. "After I cast the spell?"

Jacob shrugged. "Then you have to hope I won't kill you."

Pilate looked from Jacob's face to the chain and back. "Agreed."

Jacob relaxed his grip another few degrees but compensated for it by pressing the knife deeper into Pilate's skin. Blood trickled down onto the Roman's chest.

"You've cut me."

"I never yet saw a spell ruined by the addition of a little blood," Jacob growled. "Do it now!"

"My hands …"

Jacob stood, dragging the Roman with him and slamming the man firmly against the wall. He again pressed the dagger to the Roman, this time to his eyeball. Pilate slowly brought his hands up. Not taking his gaze from the dull gleam of the weapon in Jacob's hands, he duly chanted an opening spell, touching the chains.

Which promptly fell away.

The *Clang!* of the iron on the floor was louder than Jacob was expecting. "Again!" he snapped.

"Again?" Pilate cowered against the wall, shrinking back from the touch of the dagger. "What are you ... do you mean the door?"

"Idiot!" Jacob nodded upwards. "The window! Open the window!"

"I ..." Pilate looked up. "That will be harder."

"You're not the first wizard I've known, Roman. Do it now."

Jacob heard thudding and clanking sounds from the hall that might be soldiers approaching. So did Pilate, and he shot a hopeful eye in that direction.

"Now!" Jacob stabbed through the lobe of Pilate's ear, pinning him with a forearm across the throat in the same move.

Pilate chanted and waved, and the bars in the high window vanished.

"Prefect!"

The voice came from the door. Jacob didn't waste time looking.

He spun the Roman around by brute force and slammed his head into the stone. Pilate collapsed forward into a stunned crouch, grabbing at the wall for support, and Jacob took two steps away.

He turned and launched himself. As he heard keys rattling in the lock, he stepped onto Pontius Pilate's back, planting his feet right between the man's shoulders. He jumped, angling not at the open window, which was too high, but ninety degrees away from it, at a blank wall.

"Stop!"

Shoulders slammed into the door.

Jacob touched the wall lightly—his smashed toes *hurt*—and sprang away from it again, extending his body into the fullest stretch he could after long days of crouching in chains. The dim light of the night sky flashed before his eyes, and he feared for a moment that he was going to miss his catch—

But he jammed his left hand into the open window—

Wham!—

And held.

He swung sideways until his body was nearly parallel to the floor, his one hand straining to bear the impact, feeling the mortar crumble under the pressure. Then his swing hit maximum extension, his arm did not quite rip out of its socket, and he slid back again, under the window, still clinging.

The door imploded inward, and Jacob saw red uniforms out of the corner of his eye. The guards would have pila or javelins or something capable of reaching him.

"Kill him!"

Jacob hauled himself up with both hands. He skinned his knuckles, and the force with which he had to throw himself into the small space of the window made him bang both shoulders painfully.

Beyond the window was a drop of ten feet to a baked tile rooftop.

Pain seared the flesh of his buttock. Someone had stabbed him. But that was one thing; a spell from Pilate might do much more harm.

Jacob toppled forward.

He held the dagger out to one side as he dropped, to be sure he didn't impale himself on the stolen weapon. *Whoomph!* He hit the terra-cotta hard and felt tiles shatter under him. He slid down the roof, hands, shoulders, buttocks, and toes all in pain, uncertain of what his next step was. Whatever happened, he had already fixed on one certain resolution: he was going to start wearing boots.

At the edge of the ceiling, he crossed over a lead rain gutter, grabbed at it, missed, and fell.

Another ten feet, and he hit the ground. Dirt. Hard-packed dirt.

Jacob staggered to his feet, sucking thick air into his battered lungs and looking for a horse. They'd be after him in a moment, but he had the advantage, and he knew now he'd get away.

He was free, but he was alone, and that made him uncomfortable.

Time to go find Ishbaal and his men.

CHAPTER FOUR

Palestine

THE BEGINNING OF THE AGE OF PISCES

Get us up to the mount," Ishbaal gasped. He looked bad under the exploding lights in the sky, his white tunic and cloak soaked in blood as he leaned against the wall of the alley. Most of the blood was his own, and his dark desert complexion was drained and lifeless. His bent nose and thick, unruly hair didn't help, nor did the heavy feeling that preceded him wherever he went and crowded into his wake—the sense of perdition, gloom, and foreboding that came from the little man's surfeit of corrupt and sorcerous bargains.

"Wait here." Jacob set down his spear and stepped out into the street.

Even the street was narrow, a winding, cobbled path that climbed up to Herod's Temple between dusty yellow-brick walls.

Half a dozen paces downhill from Jacob, on a small plaza, a staved-in door gaped open. A woman's cries came from within. This morning, such cries would have meant cannibalism. The drained and depleted defenders of Jerusalem's walls were weeks beyond the ability to perpetrate anything so vigorous as rape, but as the food supplies had gone, the powerless had begun to disappear. Babies first, then children and the old, and eventually even adults.

No one talked about where they went, but everyone knew.

But this evening, under the vicious leer of the evening's first star—the last evening star of the Liminal Year—the walls had fallen, and the Romans had entered the City of David.

The Romans and their Infernal allies. With the falling shroud of night had come the Zvuvim again, and other, darker, nameless things. They had shattered the defenses with a mighty final blow, and now they chased the Judeans from door to door in the city, sparing none. Strange fire and the foul smoke of charred flesh filled Jerusalem as the powers of Hell—*some* of the powers of Hell—did their worst.

All of Jacob's men, defamed as robbers and worse, had fallen. All but Jacob himself and the mage Ishbaal. His men had fought and died for their own reasons, which included loyalty, money, and hatred of the Romans. Jacob had fought out of self-defense and a strained loyalty to his remote father— the Romans and their darker allies were after Jacob, and Jerusalem was a defensible city.

Had been a defensible city.

The three horses and the single Roman soldier standing outside the door told Jacob that the reason for the woman's screams was rather more prosaic than cannibalism, if just as sordid.

"*Ave!*" he called to the soldier as he approached. He affected a good Italic accent in his Latin and a friendly tone to his voice; that and the darkness should throw the soldier off, he thought. He just needed to get close enough to be able to kill the man quietly—

"Alert!" the man shouted. "We're attacked!"

He threw himself at Jacob.

Jacob cursed and stepped aside. The soldier pressed his assault, shouting and stabbing with his short gladius.

An answering shout from within the building reminded Jacob that there was no time to mess about. He hesitated a moment to present a better target, and when the soldier attacked this time, he let himself fall directly back.

The gladius whistled overhead—

Jacob hit the loose cobblestones and bounced—

He swept with his long legs, kicking the soldier's feet out from under him.

"*Mentula!*" the soldier cursed, and then Jacob took his own sword from the soldier's hands and stabbed it into big-nosed Roman face, right between the iron cheek guards of his helmet.

"Jew!" shouted a second man, appearing the doorway with sword in hand.

"Guess again," Jacob snarled. He rolled over the body of the dead man, coming to a seated landing with the freed gladius in his hand. The second soldier charged, evidently aiming to take advantage before Jacob could stand.

Jacob hurled the gladius.

It was long for a throwing weapon, but its tip was sharp and Jacob knew how to throw a knife straight. The gladius sank into the soldier's throat with satisfying ease, and he ran past Jacob blind and stunned, slamming into the wall on the other side of the street before finally falling to the dust.

Jacob rolled to his feet. He ached, but he had always had an excellent, athletic physique—an inheritance from his father, he thought. Ignoring the pain, he vaulted into the saddle of one of the shying horses, grabbing the reins of another as a lead rope.

A third soldier appeared in the door, bloody sword in his hand. Jacob noted with disgust that the woman's cries had ceased. The soldier stepped forward, but in a flash of light from fire streaking across the sky he met Jacob's eyes.

"You!"

Jacob charged his horse at the man. The soldier stumbled back into darkness within the building. "*Fossa!*" he swore. "Help! The northerner, bar Abbas! He's here!"

No time. Jacob turned and crossed the little plaza to the alley. "Ishbaal!" he called.

No answer.

Jacob dismounted and wrapped the horses' reins around a spar from the wreckage of what had once been some sort of merchant's tent. He ducked into the alley and found his comrade unconscious, slumped on the ground.

Bleeding and in a bad way, but alive. That was good. Without Ishbaal, Jacob had no way of opening the gate that Ishbaal was so certain was on the Temple Mount and no other way to get to the Council in time—the nearest Masseboth were leagues away, with thousands of irascible Romans blocking the path. His father worried that some of his own allies might back Semyaz's play to stay in power beyond this Liminal Year. Azazel needed Jacob's vote.

They were distant, Jacob and his father, but not so distant that Jacob wanted Semyaz on the Morning Throne.

He bent to pick up the wizard and heard a low growl.

Jacob looked up slowly. Deep in the alley, down a steep flight of uneven steps, he saw glowing eyes. Dozens of them.

Cursing, Jacob threw Ishbaal over one shoulder and grabbed his spear with his free hand. It was a good thing that the sorcerer was a small man. Two steps brought him to the mouth of the alley; he flung the little Egyptian across the back of one of the horses and jumped onto the other.

He whirled to meet the enemy.

They would have been baboons if they'd had heads. But green eyes glowed on their chests, and ragged teeth gnashed and snapped in mouths set into their bellies. They came at Jacob, bounding off the walls and leaping down from the rooftops.

Jacob charged, swinging the spear like a staff. He had to make himself a big target, he thought, and a juicy one, and not let these creatures become interested in Ishbaal. He battered one Hellbaboon against the wall, trampled two under the horse's hooves, impaled a fourth, and punched his fingers into the left eye-nipple of a fifth.

The horse screamed in panic and pain as the demons attacked it, but it had nowhere to go but forward.

Jacob flung himself backward, somersaulting over his mount's rump and landing squarely on both feet. He cracked the spear in his hands like a whip, hurling the impaled demonling off the end of it and into the body-face of a baboon that leapt at him off the wall. Another attacker he kicked twice, once between its green eyes and a second time in its backside as it turned, sending it skittering down the alley after its companions.

The rest of the monsters attacked the horse.

Jacob ran, grabbing the reins of Ishbaal's animal and leading it up the hill and away from the scene. The screams of the dying horse followed him for several minutes, and when they cut off abruptly, he guessed he was far enough away that the Hellbaboons would find some closer, easier prey than him.

He crossed through a gate into the Upper City, wishing he had some way to bar it after him. The Lower City behind and below him burned. Gigantic shadows moving from building to building and flashes of animal limbs on enormous humanoid bodies told him that some of the Fallen had personally joined in the attack.

Not the Princes, presumably. They would be at the Council. But their minions were here to catch Jacob.

For a moment, images of the fall of another city, ages earlier, flashed before his eyes.

"Not the palace, you idiot," Ishbaal murmured. He could barely raise his head off the horse's flank to look about and see where they were, and his words sounded like the distant whistle of a breeze in the trees. "The Temple."

"The other roads are blocked," Jacob said.

They crossed the aqueduct. Bodies floated in it, which didn't bode well for the path ahead of them. Even when they'd fallen to eating each other's flesh, the Jerusalemites had been smart enough not to pollute their water source.

Ishbaal slumped against the horse again. Jacob passed the old Hasmonean Palace and spared a glance for Herod's larger, newer home against the western wall of the city. The Idumaean's gaudy arriviste statement was already on fire, but the family home of Mattathias's sons lurked black and empty, looted weeks ago.

Another gate, and then long, stone stairs. Smoke thickened the air and deadened the sound of the horse's hooves clopping on the stairs. The walls around the temple precinct—where this whole doomed stand had started—loomed high and spectral, flickering green and blue and silver as sorcerous fire shattered various quarters of the city.

At the top of the stairs stood someone Jacob hadn't seen for decades.

"I know you," he said, tightening his grip on his spear while trying not to look bellicose.

"You may have known me as *Saul*," said the other man. He wore a Roman uniform and held a long club in both hands, resting it on his shoulder. It was an improvised weapon, maybe a laundryman's tool; his sword's sheath was empty.

Behind the laundryman stood a dozen Roman soldiers with swords and spears.

"No," Jacob disagreed. "That wasn't it."

Pontius Pilate's eyes flashed fire. "I'm *Paul* now," he said. He moved down one step, closer to Jacob.

"The city's on fire, *Paul*," Jacob said slowly. "Let's get out of here."

"Agreed. We'll go *your* way." Pilate stepped to one side and gestured to the Temple behind him.

"I can't," Jacob said without thinking.

Pilate's eyes flashed fire. "Fool me once," he said.

Jacob sighed. "I didn't mean it like that." He pointed at Ishbaal. "My sorcerer's dead. I don't know how to open the gate or where it is. At this point, I'm just running." He looked back at the fires below. "I don't have a plan."

"The Antonia burns," Pilate said. "But I think we can get out by the Pool of Bethesda." He stepped closer. "But first, let's get rid of this dead weight."

"No," Jacob started to say, and moved to put his body between Pilate and Ishbaal—

Pilate swung the club.

Jacob was caught by surprise. He was tired, he had fought too much already this evening, and above all, he expected any attack from the Roman to land on Ishbaal. Instead, Pilate attacked Jacob. The laundryman's club was hard and heavy, and as it slammed into Jacob's leg, he felt the bone break.

Jacob fell backward, landing hard on the stairs and sliding down. He let go of his spear in the fall and heard it clatter down the stairs and out of sight. His borrowed horse, its reins suddenly falling free, neighed and drifted upwards.

The soldiers jeered.

"Just in case you had any idea that you might want to … *kick* me."

"Wait—"

Pilate advanced, raising the club again.

"No more lies, Jacob bar Azazel," he snarled.

"Oh, yeah … *Paul?*" Jacob struggled to right himself, but the pain in his broken leg was excruciating.

"A man who lives a long time," Pilate said slowly, "may find it convenient to take many names over the years." He paused to smile, his face flickering red in the light of Herod's burning palace. "Don't you think?"

He swung his club down again, battering Jacob's other leg.

Jacob cursed in Infernal, the force of his words and his pain snapping back the Roman's kilt for a moment. Both his legs were broken beneath the knee. He wouldn't be walking anywhere for a good long time.

"I've given you your two warnings, bar Azazel." Pilate raised the club a third time. "The Liminal Year ends. The Council meets again. I *will* attend. Or you will die."

The Roman's club burst into flame. For a split second, Jacob thought that the fire was the Roman's own doing, the conversion of his mere stick into a sorcerous and even more dangerous weapon.

But Pontius Pilate shrieked and threw the club down, staring in dismay at the palms of his hands.

Jacob didn't wait for another opportunity. He hurled himself forward on knuckles and knees, grabbed Pilate by the kilt, and threw the other man down the stairs. Pilate screamed louder, but on the third bounce his scream cut off.

Jacob turned to the terrible work of dragging himself up the stairs.

The soldiers, after a moment's shock, shouted and charged.

Ishbaal leaned forward over the horse's flank, muttering something in his native Egyptian and fluttering the fingers of one hand. With the other, he slapped distractedly at the horse's tack, trying to secure himself—he slowly slid forward—missed his grab—

The Romans rushed him—

A blaze of light erupted from Ishbaal's fingers, fanning out like a blade and smacking into the entire squad at chest level. Ishbaal hit the stairs head first and crumpled. Romans flew left and right off the stairs, disappearing into the shadows under the Temple's walls.

The light snapped off.

"Ishbaal!" Jacob dragged himself to his sorcerer's side. En route, he found a pair of Roman javelins and took them with him. The rumblings and fire of Jerusalem's fall seemed remote. Ishbaal, frail and broken in his arms, was very real and immediate.

"Not dead yet, bar Abbas," Ishbaal muttered. He coughed and spat blood, as if to cast doubt on his own words. "Get me on the horse."

Jacob was relieved. He knew that the feeling of darkness around Ishbaal was something most people couldn't see. Only him. And, he thought, his father. It was the Left Hand, a seal or a claim. Ishbaal had promised himself to Hell and damnation somehow. When Ishbaal died, Jacob wasn't sure what would happen, exactly, but the man's soul would join the damned in his father's realm. "To Hell with the horse. I'll carry you."

"To Hell with the horse? That's funny. You get that sense of humor from your father?"

Jacob remembered that his legs were broken and laughed. "It isn't humor. It's stubborn pride."

"It's a fine line."

Jacob dragged himself up the side of the horse and dragged Ishbaal with him, leaning on the javelins for support. The animal objected sharply but stood still for the mounting.

"Where'd you get the horse anyway?" Ishbaal asked, bouncing slowly on the animal's back as Jacob directed it back up the stairs. The sound of Roman soldiers calling to each other as they regained their senses made Jacob nervous, but he ignored it. "I thought we ate the last one weeks ago."

"It's a Roman horse. I guess they still have cattle to eat."

"Or maybe they had a lot more horses than we did."

Jacob laughed. "And yes," he said as the horse clopped unsteadily through the gate leading into the Royal Porch, "I did get my sense of humor from my father. With his job, maybe he needs it."

"He could change jobs."

Jacob chewed on that. "I'm not sure he can." He thought again of the moment of his own death and underwater resuscitation, and the conversation he'd overheard between his father and … someone else, and his failure to ever discuss the moment with Azazel. He felt tied to his father and doomed, held at arm's length and sucked in at the same time.

What he wanted was to be free. Free and not alone. He wondered if those two states could coexist.

Ishbaal raised his head and pointed. "Deeper," he said. "Inside."

"Inside the courtyard?"

"All the way … all the way inside." Ishbaal's breathing grew shallower by the minute, and the pain lancing through Jacob's calves forced him to guide the horse by supplication as much as by use of the reins.

"You sure?"

Ishbaal nodded weakly.

"Centurion!" Pilate shouted behind them, outside the gate.

Jacob tried to make the horse go faster as they headed past metal warning plaques into the Temple courts. In the outermost gate, he risked a look over his shoulder. Beyond the Romans, in the flame-skeined darkness and chaos that Jerusalem had become, he thought he saw the familiar and loathsome outline of a tentacled Infernal.

So not all the Princes were already in the Council Chamber. He shuddered and pushed on.

The Gentiles' Court held nothing but scorched bones. Jacob felt a moment of peace crossing it, its high walls obscuring the fires consuming the city and allowing for a space of cooler air, a hollow protected from the flames and out of sight of the shadow that might have been Belial.

The Court of Women was entirely empty, and in the quiet, Jacob noticed something new and troublesome. The palpable darkness, the ill-omened feeling of trouble and sorrow that cloaked Ishbaal felt heavier. It felt closer, like it was invading Jacob's body too, into his lungs and blood and heart.

The Left Hand was stronger. Closer.

Up a few more steps and through the Gate of Nicanor, with its marble, its bronze panels, and its gilding above the door proper. He shut the Gate behind him, wishing again that he had some way to bar it. The Court of Israel, the Court of the Priests. Jacob spurred the horse as best he could with his knees, fearing the growing sensation of the Left Hand's grip and the sound of sandals in the courts behind them.

Herod's temple towered above them. There, between the altar and the door, stood a whip-thin, dirty rabble of the Zealous. Zechariah stood at their head, naked sicarius in his hand.

Jacob's heart sank.

With a dull *boom*, he heard the Gate of Nicanor open at his back.

"Are you a priest, bar Azazel?" Zechariah sneered. The Left Hand lay heavy on Zechariah, too. Heavy and ugly.

"I'm an angel," Jacob said. His legs screamed at him. "Today, we all are." He nudged Ishbaal, and the sorcerer twitched slightly in answer.

"Angels are not permitted to enter the House of the Lord."

"Herod's House," Jacob disagreed. "Soon to be desecrated and burned."

"True. And once it is nothing but a ruin, you may enter at will."

Jacob looked at the line of fanatics and felt the death of hope. They stared at him with glittering faces, hands and weapons twitching. They knew their end had come, and they planned to buy their places in Heaven with their lives. Jacob wondered if their plan would work.

He heard Roman boots behind him. He could feel the horse under him sagging from its double burden.

"Didn't David take refuge in the sanctuary and eat the Bread of the Presence?" he asked, trying one last time.

"I have no time to waste arguing with an ignorant, blaspheming foreigner." Zechariah spat on the ground.

Jacob hurled one of his javelins. It struck the leader of the Zealous in the center of his chest. He crumpled to the ground, looking surprised. The sudden increase in the strength of the Left Hand had made it feel as if Jacob were being pounded into the ground, but then, abruptly, it eased.

Zechariah twitched once, then lay still.

"Nor do I." Jacob stabbed the tip of his other javelin into the horse's rump.

Zechariah's dagger-wielding followers rushed forward. Roman soldiers attacked from behind.

But the stolen Roman horse, exhausted, spooked, and in pain, bolted. It took a sword wound to the chest as it battered its way through the Zealous, leaped up the temple steps, and charged into the darkness within.

A first chamber flashed by, and then a long hall of darkness thick with the smell of myrrh. At its end was a curtain at the top of a short flight of stairs, ten cubits tall, maybe. Something glowed or burned behind the curtain, which shimmered gold and mysterious above Jacob, Ishbaal, and the galloping, frantically neighing horse.

Then the horse struck something.

Hot coals showered both men and the animal, and they fell down together. Jacob heard the snap of bones breaking, and then the horse began to scream.

Had he run into a censer?

"Ishbaal?" No response. Jacob rolled to his knees, scattered stinging, sweet-smelling coals from his body. His shattered legs ached and almost dragged him down again. He raised the javelin over his head to put the thrashing horse out of its misery.

"Stop!"

Jacob hesitated. "The horse is dead regardless."

"Yes," Ishbaal said slowly. He was a man-shaped outline of black crouching against a field of red coal-stars on the floor. "But it matters how it dies."

Jacob heard a *snick* of metal in the darkness. Outside, *clangs* and shouting. "Hurry," he said.

"I'm going to do this thing," the sorcerer told him. Jacob felt as if the Left Hand were choking the life out of him. "You get up there and through that curtain. The Morning Throne is behind it."

"It is?"

"It will be."

"I'm not leaving you."

Ishbaal chuckled. "Oh, you'll see me again."

Jacob hesitated.

"It matters how it dies!" Ishbaal snapped. "Get going!"

Jacob crawled. Every inch his mangled shins banged across the floor yanked another curse from him. He cursed Zechariah, Pilate, Belial, even his father, and certainly himself and his own damned fate. He was at the foot of the stairs when the horse's screams stopped. He was halfway up them when the Romans burst into the door at the other end, torches held high.

"Kill the Egyptian!" Pilate shrieked.

Ishbaal bellowed a defiant curse in his native tongue.

The Left Hand squeezed once, then ceased.

Jacob leaned forward and fell against the curtain—

It caught him and held him, firm as any wall. Behind it, the light pulsated, taunting him.

"Father!" he cried. "Father, if you can see me, I need help! Open this gate, or I will not make the Council!"

"Seize the Jew!" a Roman voice shouted, and sandal soles pounded across the tiled floor.

"Father!" Jacob cried again, and slammed his fist against the curtain.

The soldiers raced closer.

"Father!" Jacob's cheeks were wet, and he wasn't sure why. Was he weeping for Ishbaal? For himself? A profound terror, a sense of isolation, swamped him, blotting out the excruciating pain in both his legs.

He raised his fist to pound on the curtain a final time, and it suddenly gave way, pulling him through and into the light beyond.

CHAPTER FIVE

Hell

THE END OF THE AGE OF PISCES

Within the gates, horror.

This was not home, it never had been. Jim (Jacob, then) had died choking in effluent in the canals of Ainok, and when he had reawoken, strange and unexplained dreams aside, he had been in this place. But in a quieter corner, ministered to by servants who were monsters but loyal and even loving.

Only later had he learned that his father's mansions were full of this new thing, the *damned*. Later still, he had come to hate the fact, and he and his father had parted. This train of thought saddened him, and he tried to force his mind down other paths. Learning to play the lute from Elaine on a rare sunny spring morning in the woods outside Crannock Castle. Warm sun spilling down her hair and dress, infinitely long and infinitely warm, a cocoon of laughter surrounding them.

"This place could really use some music," Mike said. "You know, drown out all the noise."

The noise was mostly ear-shattering screams, though if he focused closely, Jim could also hear low moans and gibbering beneath the falsetto shrieks. Beneath that, the fleshy sounds of wrestling and physical lust, the rasp of saws on bones, and the soft sucking sound of flowing blood.

The damned heaped upon each other, passionately, angrily, vindictively, greedily, two self-gnawing piles of flesh and venom split down the middle by a snaking path. It was Baraqyel's role, traditionally, to bring visitors down this path, but Baraqyel was occupied, and Jim knew the way.

The dead and damned, of course, came in by a different door and were led by minions whose presence was altogether more dispiriting.

"You're forgetting your basic principles," Eddie said. There was something different about the guitar player's face, but Jim couldn't figure out what it was.

"What?" Mike pulled a flask from his pocket and took a sip. He kept patting his pockets as he drank, like he was looking for something else. Probably forgot that he'd thrown his candy bars at the Baobab Tree. "Place gives me a baritone guitar feel. Just because Satan can't hear it doesn't mean I wouldn't feel better for a few loud chords right now. Loud and distorted."

"Yeah," Eddie admitted. "So would I."

Qayna dismounted and led her horse. Twitch swayed, then gripped the horn of the saddle tightly with both hands. Jim had never seen the fairy so battered. He wondered if it would die, but it continued to cling tenaciously to life and the saddle, staring wide-eyed around itself into the mounds of the damned.

"I knew your brother," Qayna told Jim as they passed under jagged stalactites into a new gallery. Other passages led off in various directions, but Jim stuck to the path he knew was the shortest route. All the caverns were lit with reddish-yellow light from no apparent source. Magic.

Jim suppressed a laugh. "Yeah?"

"Yes." The Marked Woman grew quiet. "I … I killed him, actually."

Jim looked at Qayna and tried to keep a poker face. She had made the wrong inference. "I thought you were famous for killing your own brother."

Qayna, the first murderer, laughed. "I've killed a lot of people," she admitted. "Most of them on purpose. Your brother was an accident, but I'm sorry."

Jim shrugged. "I grew up an only child. I don't think my father holds anything against you. I certainly don't."

"Perhaps not. Still, I have not seen him for several millennia."

"The first kinslayer and the first rebel." It was Jim's turn to laugh, and his laugh was bitter. "Estranged."

"We've walked separate paths."

Jim heard his own story in her words, and it made him feel a little better. A little. "And now? Are you really here just for the fun?"

"No. He sent for me."

The wailing of the damned sounded louder.

"Does he want you to attend the Council?"

"I don't know." Qayna was silent for a moment. "I have once before, you know. A long time ago."

"Oh yeah?"

"I was asked to vote on … an issue."

"On who would be leader?"

She looked at him sharply. "How did you know?"

"President of the Infernal Council? Lucifer? Satan? Moloch? The Accuser, the Adversary? It's the thing they care about most. It used to be the only thing they debated, until they agreed new rules and restricted when the issue could be brought up."

"Restricted it how?"

"The Liminal Year between each Age begins and ends on an equinox. On each of those nights, the Council meets, and the position of Moloch is a permitted subject for motions and debate."

Qayna looked away into the writhing distance. "The Liminal Year, when all things are possible. The equinox is tonight."

Jim nodded.

Qayna exhaled, a silent whistle. "Of course."

"I gather you haven't been an avid follower of Infernal politics."

She shook her head. "I've been too busy trying to die. But why two consecutive equinoxes?"

"That's my father's idea, I think." They crossed a stone arch, a natural bridge over a pit full of bloodied children and adults, alive with the sounds of gnawing teeth. Jim couldn't tell who were the eaters and who were the eaten. "If the Council makes a mistake, it can fix it a year later."

"But if they don't fix it then, they're stuck for two thousand years."

At the end of the arch, Jim led them right and around the base of a rockslide of boulders the size of houses. The ceiling disappeared into glowing red infinity.

"Yeah, well, if you let them fix it any time they wanted … again, they wouldn't talk about anything else."

"What would a mistake be?"

Jim laughed, trying not to sound bitter. "In my father's eye? Electing anyone other than himself."

Qayna hesitated. "I never knew him to be petty."

"Not petty," Jim agreed. "Supremely confident."

"Perhaps he has reason to be."

Jim nodded. "Semyaz held the Throne once, for a year."

"How did that go?"

Jim blinked away images of Herod's burning palace. "It was a rough year. Semyaz is a liar and a bully." He laughed. "Even more than the others."

"And what if the elected Satan dies?"

"The Fallen don't die."

"Is killed."

Jim steeled himself and managed not to look at Qayna's pistol. "There are precious few things capable of doing that."

"Precious few are not zero. What would happen?"

"I don't know, but there must be a lawyer around here who can answer your question. Why do you ask?"

Qayna looked around. "A lawyer?"

"After all, we're in Hell."

"I ask," she said slowly, "because I begin to wonder what I have really been called here to do."

They walked in silence for a while.

"I don't remember the road being this long," Qayna observed.

"Hell expands daily," Jim told her. "It probably *wasn't* this long the last time you passed this way. Damnation is a growth industry."

Eddie snorted. "That figures." Jim realized what was different about the guitar player: his bad eye, the one that always slid around crazy in its socket because Eddie had visions of Hell, wasn't bad anymore. It looked as fixed and normal as its mate.

"Where's Adrian?" Twitch asked. The fairy looked agitated.

"In this giant place, you think we have any chance at all of finding that poor son of a bitch?" Eddie sounded dismissive, but the way he looked over his shoulder as he spoke made Jim think he was uncomfortable at the thought of meeting the wizard's shade.

"In this giant place," Jim said, "if Adrian's here, it's probably inevitable that you'll meet him."

Qayna looked at him sharply.

"What do you mean?" The fairy licked its lips.

"That's the way Hell works." Waves of memories crashed on Jim's mind, and he struggled to ignore them. "If there's any possible way your past can torment you, it will shove that past in your face."

"You mean Hell will bring Adrian here to torment me?" Twitch asked.

"Or to torment him."

"Shit." Eddie adjusted his grip on the shotgun and looked around him.

"You surprised?"

"Not really."

"Unless Adrian's not here," Jim added. "Hell isn't for everyone."

Eddie stopped and looked around. "Where's Mike?"

Jim and Qayna stopped too. The cavern they were in was full of sliver-thin poles running from floor to ceiling. The poles ran through strings of human beings, impaling them like so many chunks of meat on shish kebabs. The people, naked and filthy, clawed and shouted and spat at each other, demanding space, trying to get higher on the poles, or resting elbows and knees on their neighbors.

No sign of Mike.

"Dammit," Eddie grunted. "It's like being the driver of the short bus. Every time I turn around, one of the kids is climbing out the window."

"The Mare will find him." Qayna patted her horse's neck and whispered something in its ear. The animal leaned forward and snuffled at the path with large nostrils.

"By smell?" Eddie gestured around him at the writhing, battling bodies of the damned. "In all this?"

Qayna cocked an eyebrow at him. "The Mare followed your van by smell from New Mexico to Kansas."

Eddie shut up and stood aside.

The black horse moved quickly, nose to the ground. Qayna followed at its shoulder, holding its reins gently, and Twitch clung to the saddle like a shipwreck survivor on a bit of flotsam.

The party moved back through a couple of caverns the way they'd come, and then the horse turned onto a different path. Past the pile of fallen boulders and the stone arch, it took them down a twisting gullet of green stone, through a room pocked with pits full of mud and scorched, howling souls, to a broad shelf of stone above an apparently bottomless chasm.

On the shelf, talking to another man, stood Mike.

The Left Hand had always been heavy on the bass player. It had never felt as heavy to Jim as it did know.

The other man was young, maybe a teenager. He had the lean, muscular look of a restless poor kid with no job, no likely prospects, and access to free weights. Like many of the other inmates of Hell, he dripped blood and his skin hung in tatters.

And he looked a lot like Mike. He could've been Mike's son.

Qayna stopped the Mare. "What is this?" she asked Jim.

"I don't know." Jim considered. "Wait a moment."

They watched, Eddie cursing under his breath. It was a good thing Eddie didn't speak Adamic, Jim reflected. He'd shatter the windows in every storefront he passed.

Mike offered the damned man his flask. The man refused and spat blood on the stone. Mike nodded, said a few soft words with a sad expression on his face, and tried again. The weight lifter crossed his arms and stared. Mike nodded again, slowly. He set the flask on the floor between them and opened his arms wide.

The weight lifter hesitated. He stared more. Then he stooped, picked up the flask, and took a long drink.

He wrapped his arms around Mike in an embrace.

And then the weight lifter was gone.

The flask fell to the ground with a rattle. Mike's arms squeezed around his own torso for a moment, and he stumbled. When he regained his balance, he looked around, shaking his head as if coming out of a deep sleep.

He saw the flask.

He bent over, picked it up, and hurled it into the crevasse.

"Holy shit," Eddie commented. "What the hell just happened?"

"Holy shit indeed." Jim stared at Mike.

The Left Hand was gone.

So it was possible. His father had lied. Jim's heart beat faster, and he took deep breaths to calm himself. His plan wasn't insane.

Mike walked over to rejoin them. His steps were unsteady, and he looked at his own arms and belly over and over.

"You okay?" Eddie asked.

Mike's eyes ran a little wild in his head. "Get me out of here," he said.

"First things first!" Eddie snapped. "Don't you want to get your own back? Help your brother?" He waggled Azazel's hoof fragment at the bass player as a reminder.

"*Hijo de putas*," Mike swore. "*Maricón que seas*, I guess I got no choice."

"Spoken like a true brother," Eddie harrumphed. "Now let's go get a seat at the table."

Jim turned them back to their previous path.

Far away in the bowels of Hell, a *CLANG* echoed. In its wake came the roaring of beasts.

The gate had fallen, Jim realized. He wondered how Baraqyel fared.

"What's the plan, Jim?" Qayna asked. She looked unconcerned.

"What's *your* plan?" he countered.

"I don't know. I think I'm here as witness."

"Witness to what?"

"To whatever you're going to do."

Jim laughed. "I don't know what I'm going to do," he said. "I know what I want, and I know what cards I have to play."

"The hoof?"

"Jim doesn't have that anymore," Eddie shot at her. "*I* do."

Jim nodded. He didn't think he needed the hoof anymore. Really, the hoof belonged to a different plan, one that had ended only hours earlier but now seemed centuries away. The plan had always been what he'd told the band: get the witch in Chicago to summon Jim's father and strike a deal.

Only once he'd found the hoof fragment and put it into play this close to the beginning of the Liminal Year, his father's rivals had jumped into action. They'd wanted it like they'd wanted him—for the leverage they could get at the Council's meeting tonight.

At a blasted-out bar called the Silver Eel in Kansas City, Jim had turned the tables.

But the hoof might be enough to get Eddie admission, and maybe that would still work to Jim's advantage.

At a pair of roughly-carved stone columns, their surfaces creeping with animal figures and Primal glyphs, two figures waited: Ishbaal the sorcerer and Zechariah, leader of the Zealous.

Each with a dagger in his hand.

The roaring grew louder.

Ishbaal grinned. "It's been a while, boss," he said in Latin.

Zechariah slashed the wizard across the throat with his knife. Blood spattered the gravelly path, and the wound quickly closed again to Ishbaal's natural, nut-brown skin.

"Shut up!" the fanatic shouted in Aramaic. Ishbaal plunged his own dagger into the other man's belly. Again, the gout of red sputtered quickly to a trickle and then shut off, neat as any spigot.

"Aw, Hell, no," Eddie complained. "This is *not* gonna work for me."

"I thought you were used to seeing the damned," Jim said.

"Yeah. What I don't like is the private conversations. Especially not here."

"What do you want, language lessons?" Jim asked him. "All my wizards are dead."

"Tell them to speak English," Eddie grunted.

Jim arched an eyebrow. Eddie shifted from one foot to the other, looking nervous. "These guys have been dead two thousand years, Eddie," Jim pointed out.

"I can do this." Qayna muttered a quick incantation in Adamic and blew into her fist. She then rapped once each on the foreheads of Eddie and Twitch. When she moved to rap on Mike's face, he pulled back.

"*¿Qué me haces, chucha?*" he snapped at her.

Eddie looked at his bass player through slitted eyes.

"This will make you understand," the Marked Woman said.

"Yeah? That'd be a good trick." But he dropped his resistance and let her knuckle his forehead.

"You're here for the Council," Ishbaal said. He raised his dagger, a hooked and recurving thing of Nilotic provenance, in an attempt to parry the coming blow. He failed, and Zechariah shoved his sicarius into Ishbaal's eye.

"Don't talk." Jim raised a hand. "Yes, of course."

"She's waiting for you, defiler." Zechariah's leer was made more gruesome by the blood that spattered his chin as Ishbaal shoved his recurved blade into Zechariah's belly.

"Stop talking!" Jim motioned to the band members and Qayna. "Go," he told them. "Get past these ... men."

"How is understanding this *mierda* supposed to help me?" Mike whined. "*¡Ándate a la chucha!*"

"No kidding." Eddie eyed both dead men with suspicion and clutched the shotgun and the hoof fragment tightly as he walked between them. "I'm feeling pretty good about not taking Latin in high school now. Or whatever language this is."

When the others had passed between the pillars, Jim raised his hands in admonition again to the two damned men. "You guys," he said, shaking his head at the futility of his own gesture but feeling compelled to make it anyway, "go easy on each other. There's no damnation but what you make."

It wasn't true, of course; the two men were damned and in Hell. But maybe, Jim thought, they could show each other mercy and make it just a little bit better.

The roaring was louder; his enemies were catching up to him. Jim looked over his shoulder and saw only damned souls.

"Defiler!" Zechariah spat.

Ishbaal sliced off the priest's ear.

Jim slipped between them and into the next cavern.

The last, he realized immediately. Beyond the sea of damned souls in this last chamber was the spiral staircase leading up to the arched hall and, beyond that, the chamber where the Council met. At the foot of the stairs stood guardian minions of Hell in black plates of armor like beetles, Phthonos and Misos cracking their forked tails from side to side behind them. But the thing that made Jim quake was closer to him than that.

Every damned soul in the room—if there really were multiple souls here, and not some sort of trick of Jim's perception—wore the same face.

Every single one of them was Elaine Canning, wrapped in glowing, red-hot chains.

"Jim," he heard Eddie say. "Jim, you okay?"

He wasn't okay. He was staring.

"You are returned!" the damned Elaines hissed, sadness in their thousand eyes. "Come back to free me, have you? Come back to see your handiwork? Come back to join your efforts with those of your father's million minions?"

Jim couldn't tell if it was a joke. Was she teasing him or torturing? "Elaine," he murmured. "Is this really you?"

CRASH!

The explosion came from behind Jim, and dust and fragments of rock blossomed all around him. The Baobab, he thought, or some of the larger Wild Things. They were so big, their passage through Hell was bringing down the roof.

"Who else?" Elaine snarled, and all traces of humor dropped from her voice. "And you? Are you real or another phantom image of salvation, a mouthful of water spat at the feet of the woman dying of thirst? Is this the moment of deliverance you promised me, or have you come to put your hand to damnation's plow?"

CHAPTER SIX

Crannock Castle, the West Country

ENGLISH CIVIL WAR

James lingered in Elaine's arms, letting the fruited scent and taste of her kiss lull him into a sense that the moment was eternal. She enveloped him in her voluminous sleeves, her long skirt, her golden hair. Elaine would live forever with him, and he would never again be alone.

The soldier at the door cleared his throat politely.

"I must go," James said.

"He will not speak with me." Elaine's eyes were limpid and bottomless. "I have not heard a word from his lips since he learned of my love for you."

"But he listens. And perhaps he will listen to me, too."

Elaine nodded and kissed him a final time. Something dark brooded behind her eyes, but only a single tear showed on her cheeks. Reluctantly, James left her arms, passed through the door as the soldier opened it, and faced the man he would have for his father-in-law.

"I am master of this house, sir!" Harold Canning bellowed like a bull as he entered, but the roar was sluggish and wet, and he swayed on the creaking chair. He fixed bloodshot, jaundiced eyes on James and thrust out his lower lip, making his walrusoid whiskers quiver. His doublet was frayed and stained with the signs of incontinence, and his hose was more noticeable for its holes than for the flesh it covered. Behind him, the green curtain rustled, and James shivered. Drafty old pile of stones, Crannock Castle. The soldier closed the door behind James, shutting him in with Elaine's father and two other armed men in Canning green.

"You are," James agreed. He was dressed for the highway, with broad hat in one hand and sword and two pistols through his sash. He pulled his riding cloak back behind his elbows to keep it out of his way. "You are master of this house, and your daughter will succeed you."

Canning harrumphed.

"You should speak to her. It is not worthy of you to hold your tongue."

The old man ignored him. "Even if my whore daughter stoops to embrace you, you'll not have it. I would no more give this house to you than I would to a turd she had squatted to lay in the street! You are a man of no inheritance and less consequence!"

James sighed. *If you only knew*, he thought. He carefully kept his hand away from the hilt of his sword so as not to provoke the old man. It was an effort, given the vitriol the baronet poured out upon his own daughter. "I do not want the castle."

"No? Ha!" Sir Harold sat up several inches taller and leaned back, head cocked to one side and eyes rolling. "No, you want the *land*, do you not? I would sooner see it burned to the ground than in filthy, heretic hands like yours."

"I do not believe in the divine right," James said quickly. Too quickly. The old man squinted at him with suspicion in his eyes.

"You are a Stuart man, are you not?" His hand twitched on the arm of his chair, and James was acutely aware that behind him, at the door, stood two musketeers. "I should have had you hanged the day Charles rode into Parliament with his warrants."

"I pray you, sir, stay calm." James let his hand drift slightly closer to the weapon. He shifted his balance slightly, preparing to leap sideways at the sound of boots on the wooden floor behind him.

"You think I fear you?" Sir Harold smiled, and the curtain behind him *swished* softly. James thought for a moment that he saw something fleshy moving beyond the curtain, but he ignored it. Imagination. "Because you learned to play at swords from Frenchmen and Italians?"

He was mad, James saw. He wasn't damned, though; James could clearly see that Canning was free of the taint of the Left Hand. "Taught," he corrected the old man. "*I* taught *them* to play at swords. I learned to fight with a sword well before I ever saw a Frenchman." *And well before any such thing as a Frenchman existed, in fact.*

"Whether I speak with my daughter is none of your business, interloper! And my family has been in this castle," Sir Harold choked, "since before there was a France!"

Touché. "I do not want the castle."

"Do you know what my name means?"

"Harold?" James decided to risk a joke; it might defuse the heaviness that came with the stab and thrust of this conversation. "Is it not the name of the angel who announced the birth of the Lord?"

"Impertinent blasphemer!" Canning spat. "*Canning* is *cyning.* Did you know that?"

James had heard it before and nodded, trying not to let his weariness show in his face.

"That is *king* in the good old tongue! My ancestors were lords of Mercia, did you know that? They ruled from the Dyke to Watling Street, and no permission asked, not of Alfred, not of the Danes, and certainly not of any nameless Norman bastard who wanted to marry their daughters!"

"I am not a Norman. Or a bastard. Or nameless."

"Ha!" Canning collapsed back into his seat, foam flecking his lower lip. "And yet you would have me hold out. You would have me risk my life and my inheritance for the Stuarts who squeeze me dry. They say Charles is a skilled maker of bastards. Perhaps you're one of his."

"You call yourself a king," James ground out between clenched teeth, struggling not to grab his sword, "and yet you would throw open your doors to a rabble of costermongers and gong farmers who would saw the head off their own sovereign."

Sir Harold stared, cocked his head again, and finally lurched to his feet. He moved like an awkward marionette, like a madman whose body only caught up to the motions of his mind several seconds late. "It is not your affair!" he roared.

James exhaled smoothly to control his rage. "Elaine will not leave her home. The safety of that home is therefore my concern. Sir John does not care about you or her or your people. He will kill you or turn you out to have command of this place."

"You are not her lord. I am, until she marries."

"She would marry me." The argument had become muddied, and James regretted it. The conflicts between the two men—over the war, over James's love for the old man's daughter, and over the old man's sheer obstinate dislike for James—and Harold Canning's madness were a bad combination for clarity of communication. The urgent need was for Canning not to open the gates to Sir John Horsham's advancing Roundheads, and James opened his mouth to venture another plea—

"She'll marry a horse first, and swive me up a stable of centaur brats."

James whipped his sword from its sheath. "Withdraw your words, sir!"

Sir Harold stumbled back, knocking his chair over sideways and falling to his knees. "Take him!"

James spun sideways. His fighting reflexes, honed by centuries of conflict, wheeled him directly between Canning and his two guards at the door. The older of the two, a paunchy man with a grizzled beard, held his fire and instead drew a sword. The younger, a blond boy with a nose like an onion and beetling black eyebrows, had less discipline. He pointed his wheel lock pistol at James and fired.

James dropped to the ground as the spring-pushed wheel slammed the bit of pyrite home, showering sparks into the firing pan.

Bang!

"Aagh!" Behind him, James heard the baronet yelp in displeasure or pain. *Let it be pain*, James prayed silently, and then he hurled himself off the floor and to the attack.

The older musketeer eased forward, sword warily in front of him. The younger struggled to jam his pistol back into his sash and stumbled back.

James wasn't worried about facing two men at the same time—especially not two backwater soldiers like these—but their odds of getting in a lucky blow would decrease dramatically if he could knock one of them out of the fight.

Bad luck for the younger guardsman, who was still reaching for his sword.

James flung his hat straight for the face of the older man. He stepped back, ducking under the flying object and batting it aside with the tip of his blade.

James sank his sword into the younger man's chest. He didn't mean to disarm himself, but the guardsman reacted badly to being stabbed. He flailed and kicked, and in the moment of death, he pushed himself forward onto James's own blade.

The remaining soldier rushed James, swinging his blade.

James spun again. Out of the corner of his eye he saw Canning, who was not dead and was dragging himself back across the worn floorboards towards the green curtain. James didn't know what passage might be concealed behind the curtain; it was not his home, and even Elaine didn't know all the nooks and niches of Crannock Castle. He only hoped the old man didn't have a brace of pistols behind the curtain.

The guardsman swung for James's neck—

James twisted and jerked with his arms. By sheer force of muscle—physical strength was one inheritance he did have from the father he was reluctant to name to Sir Harold Canning, or even to his daughter—James raised the still-twitching body of the younger guardsman and used the corpse itself to parry the attack.

"God's blood!" the paunchy man snapped. He stabbed again, aiming over his friend's shoulder and trying to skewer James's head.

James shifted the body up slightly, batting aside the second attack.

"Devil's spawn!"

Of course, the old soldier knew nothing. Still, his words irritated James, and as the guardsman stepped to one side and moved to slash for James's leg, James hurled his flesh-and-bone shield straight at him.

The guards tumbled back together, the dead man bearing down the live one like a battering ram carrying away a door, and James yanked both pistols from his sash. He'd gone into the room expecting resistance and maybe worse, so the guns, both of them shiny new flintlocks, were loaded, primed, and fitted with fresh flints.

He aimed at the soldier struggling under the corpse.

"Stop!"

The door to Harold Canning's audience chamber burst open behind James, and he paused. He knew it wasn't an attack, but he also knew it wasn't a call he could ignore.

The voice was Elaine's.

James nodded. "Throw aside your sword, sir," he instructed the guardsman.

"Kill him!" shrieked old Canning. His heart pounding and his breath racing in his lungs, James imagined that the crazed old man was shouting at him.

The soldier hesitated.

James raised one pistol and pointed it squarely at the other man's head.

"James," Elaine pleaded. "Will you shed blood in my house?"

"Your father's house. Your father's choice." James pulled back the hammer of the pistol. "Always your father's choice."

The guardsman tossed aside his sword and raised his hands in surrender.

"Coward!" Sir Harold disappeared into the curtain behind his toppled chair.

James hesitated, considered hunting the old man down in his own house. If he hadn't been Elaine's father, he'd have done it. Even if Elaine had simply not been physically present, James thought, he might have been willing to give chase.

He sighed and lowered both his pistols.

Elaine grabbed the hilt of James's broadsword and braced one slippered foot against the dead man's shoulder. "Poor Andrew." She straightened out her back and slid the weapon from the dead body that sheathed it. "Not exactly Excalibur and the stone, is it?"

James scooped his hat from the floor. He'd need it. "You would make a singularly fair Arthur."

"You would make a singularly large-handed Guinevere." Elaine pushed him out the door, wiping his blade in passing on her father's curtains and pressing the weapon into James's hands.

"I would be Guinevere for your sake."

"For my sake you must fly. You tried, but he will not bend his will. We shall open our doors to the Cambridge mob."

"Should I fear your father?" They jogged down dark wooden steps. James knew where they were going, but dreaded the thought of parting and shut his mind's eye to the inevitable.

"You should. He has money, men, and hatred in his heart."

"Fly with me."

"I cannot." Elaine Canning stopped on a landing. She looked into her lover's eyes and shook her head. "This is my home, and he is my father, and whatever part of my heart does not lie with you must always lie buried here."

"You talk like a witch."

Elaine laughed and continued their descent. "Am I not one?"

"Milady?" asked another soldier at the front door of the manor house. "Sir Harold?"

They passed him without stopping. "Sir Harold commands that he not be disturbed," Elaine said firmly, and the soldier bowed his head and stepped back into his place at the top of the stairs.

Elaine led James to the stables. Rain drizzled bleakly in the courtyard, the droplets falling so slowly to earth they seemed suspended, as if the thick mud were generating itself. "I had hoped to avoid this," James said.

"And yet you dressed to ride." Elaine tapped the brim of his hat. She was not dressed to ride or even to be out of doors, but James still struggled with an urge to simply throw her across the back of his horse and kidnap her.

"I ride for aid," James told her. "Matthew Taylor's men are encamped at the head of the valley. If you will not leave Crannock, I will not leave you."

Elaine shook her head. "You risk yourself," she said. "Better to ride north, be free of me and Crannock and all things Canning."

"I can never be free of you." James studied her face as she pushed him into the shelter of the stable. "I would not wish it if I could."

"Then fly north," she insisted. "Hope for a short war and a quick reunion."

"I must protect you."

"*I* must protect *you*." Elaine jabbed a finger into his chest. "I shall tell my father you have fled into Cornwall. He'll believe it, 'royalist' that you are."

"I do not care a fig for Charles." James grabbed Elaine's hand in his.

"Nor do I. But I care many figs for you."

She kissed him, and then somehow, in a daze, James was on his horse and riding out under the portcullis of Crannock Castle. He spurred the horse without mercy, hoping he could get to Taylor's men in time, hoping they were not otherwise committed, and hoping he could get back to Crannock with reinforcements—*unwanted* reinforcements, but still—before the Roundheads arrived.

He rode into the rain- and night-darkened woods, daring robbers and Roundheads alike to look askance at him. He needed allies. Crannock was too well-placed, commanding its valley and the crossroads below it with its horsemen and guns, for Charles's friends to casually let it fall to the Parliamentarians. Matthew Taylor and all his guns would come running, and Sir John Horsham would have to withdraw.

As he rode, James also called invocations into the night.

They weren't magic. He didn't know sorcery, at least not beyond the rudiments. He could recognize spells and wardings, and maybe tamper with them slightly, but he had long ago cast his own die as a swordsman. James had seen his father's route, remaking himself and the world in the image of some dream in his mind's eye with sorcery, and in the long centuries of their estrangement, James had more than once attempted to dabble in the arts of enchantment. But James simply didn't have the gift for it. He liked to keep a wizard by his side when he could—he felt naked now without one—but he himself was not a sorcerer.

But Azazel, First Prince of the Infernals, was. James had no easy gate into Hell or to the ruins of Ainok, whence his father once ruled. A wizard, when he had one, might be able to take him there in spirit by incantations or could summon one of the Infernals, including James's father, to attend. Mab's folk had other roads they could travel, though the Queendom had long ago turned its back on Hell. There were gates—places on Earth that lay especially close to Hell—but none of them was near Crannock Castle; the nearest usable henge was leagues and leagues away.

But however many years might separate them, James was Azazel's only son, and Azazel kept an eye on him. Some power in the chief of the Fallen, or perhaps in his position, title, or Throne, gave him a far-ranging ear, and that ear often fell on James.

He begged for the attention of that ear now. "Father," he begged with chattering teeth into the cold spray on his face, "help me!"

Animals thrashed in the wet forest on either side of the road, and James pushed on. His fingers grew numb and his mount neighed bitter complaints, but he continued.

"Father!" he roared.

Wet flapping sounds in the darkness raised momentary hopes. In his imagination, he saw his father's gigantic form settling onto the road before him, batlike wings snapping to shake off the water like a whip cracking open the night.

No such thing happened. Silvery-black night, wet and cruel, stared James in the face and filled his road.

"Father!"

James reached the head of the valley hoarse and shivering. Steep hills on three sides created a gentle, bowl-shaped vale with narrow passes leading out north and east.

"No lights," he muttered. Something was wrong.

Had Taylor moved his troops?

James reined his horse to a stop. He drew a pistol and hunched over it, squinting into the cold drizzle. Dark shapes bulked immobile in the bowl. They might have been tents. Had Taylor ordered fires put out because there were Parliamentarian troops nearby? But if the camp were still occupied, some sentry should have challenged James to give a password, and there had been none.

The camp must be abandoned. Might it be a trap, an ambush?

And set by whom?

James stroked his horse's neck gently, feeling its pulse hammer through its cold hide. The animal whickered a faint objection but obeyed when James urged it left, around the edge of the forest and still within the cover of trees. Silence. The smell of wet leaves and the smushy, sloppy sound of hooves plowing through the wet carpet of the forest floor.

He'd have given a lot for a decent moon.

The horse balked.

"Easy, girl," James urged it. He was about to direct the horse to move around whatever had caused it to pull back when he saw a dull glint of metal on the forest floor. The animal whinnied in distress.

James dismounted, taking the horse's reins in his free hand and keeping the pistol in the other. Probably useless, he thought, except as a threat or a club. The firing pan had to be flooded with rain by now.

He crouched low and eased the pistol forward, prodding the darkness until he hit something that rocked when he touched it. Flesh, he thought.

"I am armed," he whispered.

Nothing.

Damnation. James shoved the pistol back into his sash and reached forward with bare hands, carefully not letting go of the horse's reins. The last thing he needed was to be chasing a skittish and abused animal about in the dark. His fingers met resistance but were so numb it took him a moment to detect anything about what he was feeling.

Flesh. *Human,* he judged as he found the corpse's fingers, *and cold.* James looked nervously out into the grayer blackness of the vale, wondering if it was full of dead bodies. *Elaine.* He had come here for allies to head off the Roundheads and defend Elaine. If Matthew Taylor and his army were all dead, he must remount and return immediately.

Then he felt the first blister. He didn't recognize it immediately for what it was, but it burst as he squeezed it, coating his fingertips with viscous ooze. And then he felt another, and, as his touch became more ginger, a third.

"Father," he muttered again. "Please help. Not for me. For her."

The horse at the end of its lead snorted, but Azazel made no apparent answer.

The body was dead, but he had to know why. James tore a strip from the dry part of his shirt and filled it with powder from his horn. Under the shying horse and the canopy of the trees, he found a spot free of dripping water, wiped dry his pistol's flint, and slammed a shower of sparks into his gunpowdered nest of cotton.

The powder flared, the cotton caught fire, and James held up the little light to see. The horse neighed and pushed back;

Jim pulled the rein tight and kept the animal in check.

The extreme mutilation meant he had no idea whether he knew the dead man or not. Blisters covered the corpse's skin wherever it was visible, rendering his face a mass of pus-filled sacs, and James choked back the urge to vomit. From the midst of the dead man's face sprouted a beak, and though they ended in hands and fingers, his arms were rubbery and boneless. More like tentacles, James thought.

As if someone had used sorcery to warp and destroy the man's body, turning it into something … inhuman. Something Infernal, in fact.

A grotesque replica of a very specific Infernal.

James's light snuffed out.

"Belial."

CHAPTER SEVEN

James lay on the wooded hill and scanned Crannock Castle. The Roundhead leaders, spooked by the sudden aerial assault of Harold Canning's head, galloped back among their ranks with much less dignity than they'd had when they'd ridden forward.

"God's wounds," James cursed again.

He'd ridden in silence back from the head of the valley. His earlier shouting for his father had left him with a hoarse, scratchy voice and a low heart. There had long been distance between them, but now he was truly abandoned when he most would have wanted aid. His father would not help him, and his lover would not leave her home—in which she was now trapped.

Trapped and maybe damned, James thought. He had seen far too many damned souls in the mansions of his father to be spooked at the thought, but endless torment was not a destiny he had ever wanted for Elaine Canning. He was too far away to tell for sure whether the Left Hand was upon her and much too far away to be able to help.

He needed to get closer. He needed to get into Crannock Castle.

"Sir!"

The voice came from behind him, and as it spoke, James heard the metallic *click* of a gun being cocked.

His sword lay pinned beneath his body. His guns were wet. He had no idea how many men stood behind him. Even if he avoided death, the sound of a gunshot would alert other soldiers, who would come running. He was defeated.

"Stand, sir!"

But that would leave Elaine alone. James's brain thundered through possibilities but found nothing it could firmly grasp. And what was Belial's role in this? Was the Infernal the guiding power behind Cromwell and his troops?

Did it matter?

"I said *stand!*"

James drew his knees under him and climbed slowly to his feet. He raised his hands beside his shoulders and wished he had a dry gun, loaded and primed.

"You are not in uniform."

"I serve no lord and ride with no army," James said. "I am a mere traveler, here by chance."

"And the men with their throats slit at the base of this hill, are they victims of chance?"

"I know nothing of them," James lied.

"Spies and assassins do not wear uniforms."

"Neither do fishmongers and cobblers."

"Are you now a fishmonger?"

"I am a traveler, as I said."

"Turn around."

James turned slowly. A Roundhead soldier in a buff coat stood in the trees, leveling a pistol at James. His coat and boots were mud spattered and stained from long use, and his hair hung down to his shoulders. He was alone, and James felt a spark of hope.

"You are no Puritan," James said, nodding at the long hair. The man didn't have the Left Hand upon him, either.

"Piss off. Look to your own faith, whatever comfort it may provide."

James nodded amiably. He wanted the man as distracted as possible when he made his move. "Please take me to your commander so I may vindicate myself."

"Give me your weapons."

"Yes, of course." James lifted his sash off his shoulder. He did it awkwardly, deliberately letting the pistols both tumble to the ground.

The Roundhead snorted his derision—

And James snapped the cloth forward.

It was an insane gamble, but James had superb reflexes and a steady hand, and in his position, anything he did was crazy. Throwing himself upon the mercy of the bloody-minded, inflexible Puritan leadership would have been the most insane risk of all.

The Roundhead squeezed the trigger of his gun—

James's sash snapped onto the top of the weapon and slid down it—

The hammer slammed home onto the frizzen, but the cotton of the sash deadened the blow, and there were no sparks.

No sparks meant no shot and no noise.

James dove forward, pulling both ends of the sash with his body as he fell. The soldier's pistol slapped into the mud beside James's shoulder as James moved from a leap into a roll, and then James kicked his heels against the man's temples and crashed to earth sitting astride his man, ankles beside the Roundhead's ears.

"Murmmph," the Roundhead objected, dazed.

James didn't trust any of the pistols or the Roundhead. The knife in his boot fairly leaped into his hand, and with a quick snick across the Adam's apple, James killed the scout.

"I hope your faith gives you comfort," he said, and he thought that maybe it would. James knew from sad experience that a mortal who died with the Left Hand on him suffered in his father's mansions. What happened to all the rest, he had no idea. He had no grudge against the Roundhead soldier and vaguely hoped the man was in Heaven.

James squeezed into the scout's buff coat and sash, throwing his own aside. Carefully scraping damp powder out of both his guns, he loaded them with dry powder, tamped in a ball, and primed the firing pan. For good measure, he added the scout's pistol to his own, checking its powder to be sure it was dry. His own hair was as long as the soldier's, so he crept to the foot of the hill and stole the helmet from one of the dead sentinels, tucking his hair under it to hide it. A genuine Roundhead scout could afford to stand out from other Roundheads; James didn't want to attract any attention at all. At least, not until he couldn't avoid it. And then he'd want his head covered.

James eyed the gate of Crannock Castle once more. Elaine stood above it, staring defiantly at her enemies. The Roundheads were close. Were they too close?

And what had happened to her father?

No time to dally. James threw the dead man over his saddle and mounted. The horse moaned, and James wondered if the exertion and stress had already doomed the animal. No time to care. He rode down the hill.

Gray predawn light seeped across the narrow road beneath the knoll, turning the mud black. James joined the road and headed around the hill, away from the portcullis and the bulk of the Roundhead army.

Two men in buff coats nodded at James, and he raised his head in friendly greeting. Then they were past, and he turned off the track into the trees again. His horse shook but obeyed.

He came in sight of the men on the parapet and heard jeers. Good for them.

Crannock Castle had a moat. It wouldn't stop James from swimming across, but it would slow him down, which was what moats were designed to do. Slow him down and make him an easy target. Jumping into the moat would also end his disguise. He had to rely on the besiegers' fatigue, on his crafted deception, and on the fundamental logic of the siege: the Roundheads were here to take the castle. They'd care about lone men trying to get out because those might be messengers who would go for assistance, but they wouldn't expect a single man to try to slip inside.

James rode alongside the moat. The Roundheads were disposing their long guns in range of the walls. They worked quickly, no doubt trying to get the siege weapons into place before the sun rose and made them easy targets for the men on the walls.

James saluted Sir John Horsham and his knot of men as he passed and got only a casual perusal in return. He turned and crossed the bridge over the moat. He looked up as he rode, hoping to catch Elaine's eye without having to say anything. She stared north, though—up the valley in the direction in which he'd departed. *Looking for any sign of Matthew Taylor or me*, James thought.

He took a chance and removed his helmet. Still, she didn't look.

He reached the inner bank of the moat. The portcullis was down, its fangs slammed into the earth. Behind the iron bars was a thick wooden door, also shut.

"Here now!" called a voice behind James. "What are you doing?"

"Elaine!" James shouted. He spurred his horse forward and felt its knees buckle as the animal finally collapsed.

"Seize that man!"

Bang! Bang! The Roundhead ranks fired, and James heard the snap of bullets as they chewed through the air around his head.

He hit the ground hard and rolled, trying to stay behind the body of his horse. "Elaine!" he yelled again, waving. He was beneath the parapet now and couldn't see what she was looking at, didn't know whether she'd heard him.

The horse writhed, twisting and threatening to come back upright again. "God's breath," James barked. He drew the Roundhead's pistol and fired between the animal's ears. The horse collapsed, still.

Bullets punched the castle wall behind James, stinging his face with stone chips. He grabbed the Roundhead scout's body and heaped it on top of the dead horse to make a low wall. "Elaine!" he shouted a third time, and then he leaned across the hedge of dead flesh to return fire.

"James?"

He looked up and saw her peering over the edge of the wall. He paused, not surprised at what he saw and felt, but still horrified. Dread squeezed his chest, and a cloud of impalpable darkness shrouded his eyes. The Left Hand was upon Elaine Canning.

She had murdered her father.

The dead man under James shook from the impact of bullets, and he sank down for protection.

"The gate!" Elaine cried to her men, and disappeared.

James looked over his meat shield again and saw two horsemen galloping over the bridge in his direction.

Two was just the right number. Two was the number of loaded pistols James still had.

James shot the first horse between the eyes. It crumpled in a wave of brown muscle and hide, spraying blood on the bridge and on the inner bank of the moat. Dimly, James realized that he could now see the blood as red, which meant that the light was improving. Morning was imminent.

Behind him, the portcullis machinery *groaned*, an enormous sound that James could feel in his bones.

He couldn't spare a glance at it yet. He let the second horse charge past the first and get nearer, dangerously near, before he shot it in the chest. The animal hit the ground like a cannonball, plowing across James's improvised shooting wall and knocking it all askew.

The rider screamed as the horse's body ground his leg beneath it. Without standing, James reached over and ran the man through the neck with his sword. The spurting blood looked redder than red. *Why is she damned and not I?* he thought. *I have killed many men. What has happened in the hours of my absence?*

"He's a Cavalier spy!" Sir John Horsham shouted. But he stayed behind a cannon and a low wooden palisade wall, waving at his men to attack. Roundheads left their big guns and raced forward.

James grabbed the dead horseman's pistol. The other rider rose to his feet, gun in his hand—

Bang!

James's shot threw the man's dead body into the moat.

"Run!"

The voice belonged to Elaine, and James turned and sprinted towards the portcullis before even looking. The iron grating was raised a foot and a half off the ground, its sharp spikes glaring menacingly at the earth beneath it. Behind the portcullis, inside the open door, stood Elaine Canning, a smoldering old snap matchlock in both hands.

"James!" she cried.

He hurled his sword ahead of him, then threw himself at the ground without slowing. Bullets popped in the air about him, *thunking* angrily into the wood of the castle's door. He slid on his belly, rolled, and finally tumbled to a stop beside the door.

"Drop it!" Elaine called inside, but the portcullis was already crashing down.

Jim lurched up into a crouch. Partly by the tired springs in his legs and partly by Elaine's hand on the collar of his coat, he fell through the open door and then collapsed again to the ground as Elaine slammed the door shut.

Crannock Castle's courtyard spun for a moment while James caught his breath.

"James," Elaine said, cradling him as he half rose. "I begged you to flee."

"I would have," he said, putting on his best devil-may-care grin, "only you would not come with me."

Outside the castle, cannons began to fire. Chunks of stone and mortar ripped from the parapets rained down inside the courtyard, and the manor house within lost its first window to a high-flying ball. Soldiers in Canning green rushed for the steps up to the ramparts with muskets in their hands. A few lingered, watching Elaine as if waiting for a command.

"James." She looked into his face, and her hard, brilliant eyes wavered and filled with unexpected tears. "I have done a terrible thing. Your heart may not bear it."

The morning's sun began to creep over the parapets with the gunfire, but the darkness of the Left Hand hung about

Elaine like a shroud. "I saw your father's head fly from the ramparts," he said, and shrugged, trying to make light of the burden he felt. "I nearly took it off myself earlier."

Elaine laughed, a sound that lifted James's heart with hope. "He was going to send his men after you, James. He knew where you'd gone. I had to kill him to save you, and I would do it again a thousand times. That is not all, though," she added softly. She had a sudden sadness in her voice James hadn't heard before.

He sat upright. "What is it?"

"A trade, Jacob."

The voice came from behind Elaine, and it wasn't human. It sounded like large sheets of metal being torn apart, and James recognized it instantly.

"Belial!" James grabbed his sword and jumped to his feet. The ground under him shook as a cannonball plowed into the portcullis, only a few feet away.

Belial, ugliest Prince of the Fallen, moved out of the shadow of the castle's wall and into view. He was scabby and unearthly, a mass of quivering, blistered flesh that split and split again into tentacles. He had no visible face, only a fierce beak. He looked like a cancerous octopus standing on its own head, a sentient, mutated, moving eggplant.

"Your woman has damned herself."

James ground his teeth. "Your status as a Prince of Hell limits my choice of satisfying profanity."

Belial groaned in laughter. "You could tell me to go Heaven."

"What do you want?" James scanned the tentacles closely, calculating where he'd hit the Fallen if he had to. *Inside the open beak* was the only tactic that struck him as at all plausible. The rest of Belial was just too big and soft and undistinguished looking to seem worth attacking.

"You have a right to sit on the Council, Jacob."

"I prefer to be called James now. And you have the same right. For that matter, anyone who attends the Council meeting can vote."

"But not anyone can attend the meeting. Participants must be entitled or admitted by vote."

Elaine laughed again. "I did not imagine Hell to be so much like Parliament."

"Does it not seem fitting?" James grinned at her. Another ball smashed into the front of the manor house, throwing a plume of smoke and ground-up stone across the castle's yard. The entire scene was unreal to James. He struggled to keep despair off his face.

"I have agreed to help the woman," Belial said. "She has agreed to my price."

"Price?" James hesitated. "Will you remove the Left Hand from her?"

The tentacled thing quivered in what might have been a negative gesture. "Perhaps Moloch may do that, perhaps not. I am certainly not able. But I have promised to save this place from its enemies for the price."

"What is the price?"

"Your vote, James."

"On what?" James pushed Elaine to one side gently, fearing that combat was imminent. A pall of gunsmoke scudded over the castle yard like a lid on a pot, and he struggled against the sound of the explosions to keep his thoughts in good order.

Belial was silent for a moment. "On the only thing that matters."

James snorted. "The Throne? You speak of a vote hundreds of years from now."

"I will have your word today."

James nodded to the Canning troops who stood aimlessly behind Elaine. "Take her away from here," he said. "Into the manor, somewhere safe."

"Milady," said one the soldiers. They had no reason to obey James other than fear and the astonishing input of their own senses. Those were enough. Elaine jerked an elbow away from one soldier, but two others grabbed her, dragging her away from the confrontation, loyal enough to risk her wrath.

"A new bargain," James suggested. He paced to one side, circling around Belial and putting himself between the monstrous Fallen leader and his lover. "And a new price. You leave my woman in peace, and I will leave you alone."

Belial trembled. "You do not understand. The spell has been cast, the pact made. If you will not pay the offered price, there is an alternate tariff, and your woman will pay it."

James heard disturbance in the courtyard but could pay it no attention. He continued to circle.

"I cannot vote against my father. Without him, I am alone."

"You are alone because you have power. Friendship is for the weak. Only the downtrodden have need of cuddling."

James advanced. "Undo your pact, Infernal."

Belial laughed, a sound like a burning house. "And then what? Will you sing to her in the houses of the damned to ease her pain?"

"If I must." James slashed experimentally at the tentacle nearest to him, slicing off a length two feet long.

Belial didn't bleed or cry out. He reared up, tentacles curving up and back like a scorpion's tail poised to strike. "Choose now," the Fallen hissed. "The pact is binding. The choice is upon you."

"Leave him alone!"

The voice was Elaine's, and she was shouting. James looked up and was surprised to see his lover standing on the walkway of the castle wall. She held a short musket in both hands and pointed it at Belial. The sight of her defiant pose, dress and hair snapping gold and green in a morning breeze, cheered James's heart.

"Leave him alone!" she shouted again.

Belial ignored her. "Choose," he groaned.

James looked up at Elaine and smiled. He didn't know how he'd free her of the Left Hand, but he knew it must be possible. And he couldn't side against his father—not with anyone, and certainly not with this monster.

"Go to Hell," he said.

"Not I," Belial answered, his words grinding and pounding like a blacksmith at work.

At that moment, a cannonball crossed the parapet and sliced Elaine Canning neatly in two.

James's heart stopped, and time froze in a trickle of honey. Elaine's blood and broken body fell down upon him in a grisly rain.

He was yelling, he realized. He tried to stop himself, and found that he couldn't. The taste of Elaine's blood filled his open mouth.

When his howling and weeping ended, the wall was breached, and Roundheads poured into Crannock Castle to claim it.

Unhearing, uncaring, almost unseeing, James took his sword in hand and strode to meet them.

"Belial!" he howled.

Chapter Eight

Men fell to the ground left and right under James's merciless advance. They were soldiers and competent fighters, but competent at best, and unequipped to meet a warrior of James's experience.

There were very few other warriors with as much experience as James, son of Azazel.

He plucked a pike from the hands of an advancing soldier and hurled the long, heavy spear into the flank of a horse. When the animal and its rider tumbled into a squad of musketeers, James took full advantage of the confusion, wading in with heart roaring and blade singing. Ears, throats, hearts, and more felt the bite of his sword and sank with their owners to the rocky dirt on the castle yard's floor.

Then James was through the gap and advancing into the oncoming wave.

"Canning and Mercia!" someone behind him yelled. The voice might have been a million miles away for the remoteness of the sound, and James strode inexorably forward. He snatched loaded guns from the hands of dead and wounded men when he found them, firing off shots into the Roundhead forces elsewhere on the castle wall.

He crossed the moat on a bridge of corpses, grinding dead faces beneath the heels of his riding boots.

He looked beyond and above the men he fought, his body mechanically doing the job it had trained for centuries to do without the need of any conscious input, not against this cannon fodder. His eyes and his mind ranged elsewhere, searching for the Infernal who had wrecked his life, who had stolen Elaine from him.

The morning sun was bright, but the trees grew thick around Crannock Castle, and James could not be sure of what he saw. But he thought a rustle beyond the knot of men that was the Roundhead command might be caused by the retreating Belial.

So be it. They wanted him a Cavalier and a threat, he would be a Cavalier and a threat.

"Canning and Hell!" he shouted, not sure what he even meant, and leaped into the saddle of an abandoned horse.

He wheeled the animal around and charged, catching Sir John's eye in the process. John Horsham looked surprised, and then perhaps a little pleased, to see one of Crannock's defenders make such a counterattack. James thought he heard more of Elaine's soldiers thudding across the dirt behind him, but he paid them no attention and lunged forward.

BOOM!

A cannon thundered to James's left, and he only noticed it among the hail of gunfire because at the same moment his horse exploded under him like a bladder full of blood slammed against the earth. He hit the ground awkwardly but managed to turn his movement into a forward roll that brought him into a slightly dazed crouch.

James shook his head, wiped blood from his face, and then realized that the weight of the weapon in his hand had changed. He looked at the sword and found the blade snapped off halfway along its length.

"God's wounds," he cursed. His head rang like he was standing inside a bolt of lightning. "It will have to suffice."

He stood and charged again.

Two men reloading a cannon fell to his half blade, slashed through the face in a single motion. A musketeer captain ordering his cadre to reload lost his throat, and his men fled. A burly Roundhead pushing a barrel of powder from a sheltered spot behind a knoll out to the cannons lost a hand to James's fury and fled, and then James leaped from the edge of a supply wagon into the air, vaulting onto the back of Sir John Horsham's own mount.

"Damn you, sir!" Sir John howled, drawing his poniard.

"Even so," James muttered grimly, and he slashed Sir John through his fat throat. *Damn me so I won't have to be alone.* The blubber around the Parliamentarian's neck left James uncertain about the effectiveness of his attack, so he slashed a second time and a third, and then Sir John stopped moving and James was certain he was dead. He tossed aside his own broken weapon, drew Sir John's sword from its scabbard, and hurled the Roundhead's body forward into the dirt.

Blood spattered him and the horse both. Gunfire rattled the air. A ragged wave of green was mown into nothing as it ran into the teeth of the incoming flood of buff, but James noticed none of those things. All he noticed were eyes—manic, wide, staring eyes in dozens of faces turned in his direction.

For a moment, he and the eyes all froze.

Then one eye squinted, and beneath it, a pistol raised.

"Ha!" James snapped the reins of Sir John's horse and yanked it around, turning the animal away from Crannock Castle, in the direction where James thought he might have seen Belial escaping.

He left the battle at a gallop.

Not fleeing, he told himself later, as the horse's hooves pounded over wet plain's grass. *Pursuing the enemy.*

He didn't see Belial in the pursuit, though. Nor did he see any track or other indication of the Infernal Prince. And as the sun reached its noon zenith in the sky and he heard the rumble of gunfire and the squeal of bugles from other battles, unseen behind wood and hill, he realized that he was running for the henge.

He reached the stones in the early evening, his heart still racing. A lesser man, a more ordinary mortal, would have died from the sheer adrenalin rush that continued to rage through James's body. He shook it off, released the grateful and exhausted horse, and stepped inside the standing stones, his pistols and Sir John's sword in his sash.

His knees buckled, and he almost fell.

"Baraqyel!" he roared, catching himself against an upright column like a jagged fang. "Open up!"

The scene around him changed. The sunny plain of southwest England with its faint tang of distant gunpowder on the breeze disappeared, and in its place rose two towering doors with iron knockers, opening to release Baraqyel, his father's gatekeeper.

The Infernal's birdlike feet scratched furrows into the stone as he walked forward.

"Jacob," Baraqyel said.

"James. Let me in."

"Your father is expecting you." Baraqyel didn't move out of the way.

"I wager he is. Stand aside."

Baraqyel hesitated, leaning on his gigantic spear like a staff. "You know that I can't bar the way to you," he acknowledged. "But do you really think this is wise?"

"Entering my father's house?"

"Entering your father's house angry."

James was not in the mood. "The next time you offer me unsolicited advice as to the wisdom of my actions, doorkeeper," he growled, "I will teach you the folly of yours. *You are a servant.*"

Baraqyel nodded, his long silver hair bobbing gracefully over James's head, and he stepped aside. "I am a servant," he agreed. "But remember this: I serve of my free will. I am no one's slave—not your father's, and not yours."

James trembled in rage. He almost apologized. He almost slashed at the Infernal's face as he bowed low. In the end he did neither, and walked into the throat of Hell.

He found Elaine. Hell brought her to him in a melting, brownish grotto at the end of a path of upright nails. She wore an elegant formal dress, her hair bound in wire, and her entire body was wrapped in chains that glowed red-hot like iron in a blacksmith's fire. The stench of scorched skin sizzled in James's nose, and he had to fight not to look away.

Beside Elaine in the grotto stood her father, Harold. He, too, was dressed as if for an invitation to the Palace of Whitehall, in unblemished stockings, doublet, and a vaguely crownlike cap, as James had never seen him in life. His head was reattached and animated, and like his daughter, he was wrapped neck to ankle in smoking red chains.

Both had their arms free of the bindings. Each held, in his or her hands, the dangling end of the other's chain.

Held and pulled, teeth grinding with exertion and pain.

"Elaine," James heard himself moaning.

She looked at him, eyes glassy with pain. "James."

"I am sorry."

She didn't meet his gaze. Were those eyes blinded? "I chose," she said. "I was forced to it, but we are all forced to choose, and none of our choices is good. That is the terrible truth of the valley of the shadow of death. I do not regret that I had to choose, for I do not regret being human."

"Elaine," he moaned.

"Nor do I regret what I chose. I murdered my father, yes. I had to do that or let him murder my love. I gave my soul in pawn to the devil because I thought I could have my family's home."

"Belial," James rumbled.

"I do not regret that, either. I chose the deed; I accept the punishment."

"Someone else," James said, trying to formulate an objection. "Someone else could …"

"But I do regret, love, that I cannot be with you."

James grabbed Elaine's hand, tearing it away from the red-hot chain. Blackened, scarred flesh, pus, and patches of uncovered bone stared up at him for a brief moment before she snatched her hand away again and seized the chain. As if in rebuke, her father groaned and yanked harder on his end of the chain.

"I will undo this," James said. "By my self, by my soul, by my life and my father's life, I will free you from this terrible burden that I placed upon you."

"Do you not see, James?" she said, and for a moment her eyes cleared and focused on his face. "I *chose* this burden."

James stumbled away, tears streaming down his face.

"I *chose*, James!" she called after him.

James stumbled blindly among the damned, ignoring their howled regrets and their bitter reproaches. He clung to Sir John's sword at his hip like to a lifeline, though here it would do him no good. Did he imagine he would attack his father with it? His sense began to return. But he kept the sword and the pistols and doggedly ran on.

Coiled in the heart of Hell lay the Infernal Palace and a warren carved out beneath the Palace that had once sparkled at the heart of the Free City of Ainok. It was separate from the Abyss-mounted chamber where the Council met and shielded from the writhing mobs of damned souls by trusted servants.

"Phthonos." James greeted the Hellhounds at the front door reflexively. "Misos."

They growled back at him with affection, blowing jets of flame from their crocodilian nostrils that shook smoke up from their broad leonine backs in rows of black wisps, and then settled back to watching as he passed. One of the damned, a bent old man repeatedly nailing his own feet to the floor with a mallet and then ripping them out again, stumbled sideways and within Phthonos's reach as James passed. The Hound batted him away effortlessly, its massive paw knocking him head over heels back into the howling mob.

"Father!" James roared, and he filled both his hands with pistols.

Eyeless imps, many-legged crawling things, and slugs with gaping mouths scattered out of James's way. Hell was not Ainok, with its hundreds of fair concubines, its bustling markets, and its spiraling canals. Hell was howling, grim-faced servants and the business of inflicting pain.

"Father!" James pounded on the doors of the Audience Hall with the butt of one pistol.

"I'm here, son." At the end of a long hall to James's left, Azazel appeared, massive and scene dominating even with his wings furled. He beckoned to his son, then retreated under an arch that James knew opened onto a balcony in the Abyss.

James followed, wiping blood away from his face and hands again.

Azazel stood waiting for him on the balcony. The stone platform jutted without warning from the wall of the Abyss for the length of several hundred yards and then, just as abruptly, ended. It was as wide as a boulevard and had no railing. Azazel needed no railing; he had wings.

But if James fell into the darkness, he wondered, what would happen? Would he ever hit the bottom? He didn't know whether the Abyss even had a bottom. It looked like it fell forever.

What it did have was light. Sunk into the walls of the Abyss here and there in uneven patches were crystals, gems, and fungus. Trogloditic creepers, white, eyeless, and relentless, also skittered upon the face of the rock face in all its apparently infinite directions, and the troglodytes as well as the stones and the lichen glowed with reflected light.

As he had done a thousand, thousand times before, James looked up. He saw no sun, no source of light, no ceiling or end to the Abyss above any more than there was a visible end to it below. The wall glittered and glowed in patches, but it was all reflection, and James couldn't tell what was being reflected.

Thud.

Azazel tossed something onto the floor between them. He stood with his wings close in to his back, which made him as small as he was capable of appearing. His posture felt like a humble stance, despite the fact that he towered over James.

"What is that?" James asked, curiosity getting the better of him even as he looked for himself.

It was a saddle.

"You were deceived," his father said.

James knelt to look at the saddle. It was an ordinary-looking saddle, his size, and the sort he had spent many years riding. "I don't understand."

"You were deliberately ensnared."

James replaced the pistols in his sash. He turned the saddle over, still trying to figure out what his father was getting at. On the underside of the leather, a network of scratches sketched out a ward that he couldn't activate, but he recognized the Infernal glyphs and guessed at their use. "Silence," he said.

"It's your saddle," Azazel told him.

So it was. James almost laughed. "Belial," he concluded. His heart began to rise within him. His father was showing him cordiality, welcome, even warmth. Was the stiffness between them over? Surely his father would help Elaine.

"He had also warded the castle. I had no idea, and I couldn't hear you."

James dropped the saddle and stood up. "This is outrageous."

Azazel shook his head. "It is normal. The Princes of Hell play a very rough game."

"I am not a Prince of Hell."

"You are." Azazel cracked a faint grin. "You are a Prince of Hell of a different sort, perhaps, but nonetheless … you sit in the Council by right, and you are my son. To Belial, this makes you fair game."

"A game is played with rules."

"Not this one. Or at least, not very many rules."

"To attack my love … ?"

Azazel turned and looked into the glittering Abyss for a long time. "What do you think happened to your mother?"

James had no answer.

Azazel looked long into the shaft of light that pierced the center of Hell.

"You handled Belial perfectly," he finally said. "You did not tie yourself to him as he wanted. He would have had you oathbound to serve him at the Liminal Council, to vote to depose me. Your refusal was the right choice, son. If you made it for my sake … I must thank you."

"Was it the right choice?" James's head spun, and he took deliberate steps away from the edge of the balcony and the Abyss. "But I damned her."

"The alternative was worse."

James leaned against the cold stone wall of the Abyss. He ignored a glowing white centipede that crawled over his hand and tried to think.

"Why?" he asked.

"This office carries a lonely burden." Azazel spoke slowly. "None of my rivals understands that, none of them is … suited."

"Not suited because Belial doesn't understand?" James flailed. "Understand what?"

"Consequence," Azazel said. "Remorse. Wisdom. Hell is not just punishment."

"Elaine now suffers the consequence of my failure!" James snapped. "This is a perversion! What will she regret—love? Will that make her *wise*?"

Azazel studied his son. "Perhaps she will regret murdering her father. Perhaps she will regret choosing pride in her ancestral home over life." He shrugged. "Perhaps, even, she will regret consorting with one of the Princes of Hell."

"I am not a Prince of Hell!" James roared.

His own voice echoed back at him from the Abyss, progressively more hollow at each fainter return.

"What will you do?" he asked his father when the echoes had died down.

"I have already created a nasty snare and lodged Belial in it. He finds himself in the fragmented wilds of Mab's Queendom in a labyrinth of my making. I think it will take him some years to escape, and if he encounters Mab's folk, he will learn to his regret that they are not fond of trespassers."

"And for Elaine?" James's heart hammered large and loud. "I have stood by you against your enemies. Will you stand by me? What will you do for Elaine?"

Azazel, First Prince of Hell, sighed. "For Elaine, I will fulfill my appointed role."

James ground his teeth, biting back disappointment and rage. "What does that mean? You'll torture her?"

"I'll allow her to torture herself."

James shook his head. "And then what? What is the end?"

"I don't know," Azazel admitted. He turned and looked pointedly out into the Abyss, infinite above and below and sparkling with mysterious light. "Perhaps there is no end."

"That's no answer!"

"It's the only answer I have. I'm sorry. If you are looking for the mechanic of the universe, the great engineer who understands the entire system and knows its purposes and final states, you are in the wrong palace. I am a lawbreaker—not the first to break the law, but the first to willfully rebel, and I am here to serve out my sentence as best I can." He gestured at the arch behind James and the damned beyond. "I do it because I must, and I do it … for them. I will do it for her."

"Release her from damnation."

"I cannot."

James pulled his pistols again. Fury pounded in his temples, and the guns felt ridiculous and tiny in his fists, but he pointed them at his father anyway. He wanted to tell him about lying under a pool of water, frozen and dreamlike, seeing fire and hearing his voice. But he couldn't. "Impossible."

"But true."

"You sit on the Throne. You're Lucifer, first of the Princes of Hell. Moloch. The Adversary and all that."

"I run this part of the machine, no more."

"Free her!"

"Son …" Azazel reached forward gingerly.

"No!" James pointed the trembling pistols at his father. "You release her, or I won't come back as your son."

"Don't do this."

"I'll be done with you. Not cordial, not estranged. I'll be your enemy. If I am a Prince of Hell, I'll act like one. I'll come back with an army, with weapons and power, and I'll make you do what I want."

"But I can't. I don't have the power." Azazel's words echoed softly off the rock face.

"I'll make you!" James was blind with fury, and he had no idea what he was saying. All he could see in front of him was

Elaine, bound in red-hot chains and blaming herself for what he had done to her. "I'll make you, or I'll do it myself!"

Bang! Bang!

James fired both pistols into his father's chest, knowing he could inflict no injury, and hurled the guns to the ground. Azazel's great brow furrowed into a thick knot as the gunsmoke blew about his face. He opened his mouth as if to speak but then closed it again.

And looked down at the ledge on which he stood.

James turned and stormed out of the Palace and then out of Hell.

CHAPTER NINE

Hell

THE END OF THE AGE OF PISCES

It's not Elaine, Jim told himself. *If it were, she'd be here with her father.*

He didn't believe it, but it didn't matter. She was somewhere in his father's mansions, and in any case, the roaring and crashing behind him meant he was out of time.

He pushed past her, his own flesh stinging at contact with the hot iron of her chains. Qayna came with him, urging her monstrous horse into a trot, Twitch still clinging to its saddle. Eddie and Mike scrambled to keep up.

Two minions in beetlelike armor at the foot of the stairs scuttled aside and turned the blades of their pole arms away to let Jim pass. Beyond them, the dozens of similar guardians thronging the steps rustled left and right, parting like a curtain of chitinous armor. A sharp click behind Jim as he leaped up the first three stairs told him that not all his companions had been allowed through.

He turned.

"No right," one of the guardians hissed. The foremost of them held their halberds low and between them, crossing to block the way to Mike, Eddie, and the Marked Woman.

"I'm invited," Qayna said, and she brushed aside her long black duster to show the pistol at her hip and the knives strapped to her legs. Jim remembered the shots she'd fired at the surrounding Bearers of the Sword on the rooftop of a meatpacking plant in Dodge City and the red blooms like blood that had spouted from the impossibly wounded angels, and he himself flinched.

The sentinels either didn't recognize the weapon or they were braver.

"The Child of Mab has no right." A dry, rotting smell wafted from their mouths as the guards spoke, and Jim thought he saw mandibles twitching at the margins of their faceplates. These were minor minions of Hell, and he'd never seen one of them out of its armor. If they had names, he didn't know them. For all he knew, they didn't exist out of their armor.

Twitch looked up at the rider and then at Jim. "Please," it said, face pale and twisted with pain. "You can't leave me."

Jim looked beyond Twitch at the thousand damned Elaines and forced himself to steel his heart. "Take her," he said to Mike, ignoring the fairy's plea.

Mike did it, the fairy looking small and frail in the bassist's arms. His face cycled through emotions Jim couldn't read, and then he looked up at the singer. "Me too, huh, *maricón*? You just gonna leave me like a piece of shit on the sidewalk? You guys said come along, and now you're just gonna screw me worse than I was already screwed?"

"Don't worry," Jim said. "I get what I came for, I can help everybody." It was at least half a lie. The Left Hand that had hung around Mike since Jim had first met the bass player in New Mexico was gone, and Jim wasn't sure Mike needed help anymore. "It won't take long, and besides, nobody's after you. Just get in a corner and keep your head down."

Mike spat on the ground, but he stepped aside. Phthonos growled at the chunky bass player, jetting smoke from the nostrils on the top of its leathery snout.

"You leave your churls with me?" Elaine shouted at Jim in astonishment, the words echoing from dozens of mouths. He tried not to look at her. Soon, somehow, he would give her solace. He had to believe it. Mike himself was the proof. Mike was a thumb in his father's eye, a refugee from damnation.

It must be possible for others to escape the Left Hand.

"I ain't staying behind." Eddie raised the hoof fragment in his hand and stared at Jim. "I got a right too."

"No right," hissed the sentinels.

Qayna raised an arm and pointed at the back of the hall. "You have bigger problems, soldier."

CRACK!

Chunks of stone as large as Jim's head burst from the far wall like popping kernels of corn, hurtling into the room. Qayna yanked the reins of her horse and turned the animal, sheltering Mike and Twitch from the rubble with her mount's broad, black flank. Jim and Eddie ducked, and Jim staggered as the cloud of rock slammed into him. A wave of stink rushed into the chamber, hotter and more fetid than the air already inside, and with it came buzzing demonic flies the size of wolves.

"Go!" Eddie shouted, and he leaped forward.

Beetle soldiers grabbed him and hurled him to the ground.

Jim hesitated, taking in the scene.

Qayna whispered to her horse and slapped its rump; the beast followed Mike as he carried the battered fairy into the corner of the chamber. Eddie kicked and punched like the champion hand-to-hand fighter that he was, but the demonic guardians of the Infernal Council's privacy were relentless and willing to take large amounts of pain. They piled onto him, grasping, biting, and pummeling with the butts of their pole arms. Eddie howled in wordless irritation.

Phthonos and Misos leaped forward, through the scattering mob of damned Elaines. As the wall facing them sagged and collapsed, the invaders rushed in. Beaked Belial and the glowing white Raphael loomed above the ogres, Baalim, and warped beasts around them, but towering ever higher than them, frustrated in its attempts to enter by the lowness of the cavern, was the Baobab. Only its mobile, leg-like roots were visible, but it slammed repeatedly into what remained of the wall, shaking rubble down out of the ceiling.

Below the giants came Mab, regal and angry with spear in hand. Oberon sprinted beside her in the dust, bounding on all fours like a rabbit with long green coattails flapping out behind him. Rangers accompanied them, ragged and battered but doggedly shifting shape and trading blows with Azazel's minions. Pontius Pilate, the Legate of Heaven, rode something that might have been a millipede but for its size and the scabby, featherless wings that stretched left and right above and behind him, sheltering him from the worst of the chaos. His galero had been knocked off somewhere in the bowels of Hell, and the dusting of powdered stone over his red robes made him look pink. In a less turbulent moment, Jim might have laughed at the sight of him.

Around them all, in a chittering angry cloud, swarmed the Zvuvim.

"Run!" Qayna yelled at Jim. She grabbed his elbow as she sprinted past him, pivoting him on his heels and turning him in the direction of the top of the staircase. Beetle-esque fighters rushed down the steps past Jim, and behind him he heard Misos and Phthonos barrel into fiery action.

ROAR!

"Jim!" The yell was in Eddie's voice.

Jim turned to look. Eddie was bloodied and covered with swarming Infernal warriors, but he wasn't beaten. The shotgun had been ripped from his hands, and he fought now tooth and nail—the nail being the fragment of Azazel's hoof, which he slammed left and right like a sharpened fighting staff, shoving it into slotted visors and up beneath chin plates to wound his attackers.

"Jim!" Eddie called again. He jerked his head to one side to avoid a crashing bootheel, and his wild, staring gaze caught Jim's eye.

Jim felt like a snake. He would help Eddie, he told himself, he really would. He had intended to all along. Eddie wanted the Left Hand lifted from him, and once Jim knew how to do it for

Elaine, he'd do it for Eddie, too. But he had to get to the Council meeting to do anything, and he couldn't get bogged down. The hoof had once been the linchpin of his plan, but he had never been all that certain it would work—his father was a powerful sorcerer—but Jim had a better tool now.

"Jim!"

Belial surged forward, the blobby, wormlike avocado bulk of his sorcery-twisted body hurling Misos aside and plowing through beetle soldiers and buzzing Zvuvim alike. Mike huddled in the corner with the shattered fairy Twitch. The bass player had his pistol out and pointed it around wildly, but the gun wasn't what kept him safe. The Marked Woman's flesh-eating horse reared up over them, lashing out with its front hooves at any creature, Infernal, fairy, or other, that got too close.

Jim turned his back on the band and ran.

Up the stairs on Qayna's heels he rushed. The infinite caverns of Hell spewed minions from holes in the walls he couldn't count, pouring along the walls, onto the stairs, and even scuttling across the rough-hewn ceiling. They rushed, weapons first, towards and past Jim, parting around him. He encouraged them with his broadsword, knocking aside any armored Hell-thrall that threatened to get under his feet. They hurled themselves on the flies, at the Rangers, and under the crushing bulk of Belial and the Wild Things.

At the top of the stairs, Qayna turned and kept running.

At the edge of leaving the large cavern thundering with the sounds of battle, Jim paused.

The Marked Woman's boots thudded heavily down a colonnaded hallway that Jim had walked down thousands of times. The arches let in the glowing, million-sourced light of the Abyss, some of it crosshatched by gratings or tinted by colored, translucent panes. The hallway was free of the minion-fueled chaos that raged at Jim's back. The feeling that stopped him wasn't fear, exactly … it was something more subtle than that, something he had a hard time putting his finger on.

When he had entered the Council chamber before, he finally realized, it had been as his father's son, to cast a supporting vote to try to keep Semyaz away from the Morning Throne, and then again, when that had failed and Hell and Earth had both suffered a tumultuous year under the heel of the boar-headed Fallen, to cast him out of it. The tightening in his gut that paused him now was a sense that he was about to do something drastic and that everything was about to change.

Drastic, and maybe rash.

CRASH!

Jim threw himself aside as something slammed into the wall beside him. He backed against the wall, sword out to defend himself, and found himself standing beside the lion-sized body of Phthonos, one of his father's hounds—the one that had nearly caught up with him in Dudael, New Mexico, in fact.

Phthonos whimpered. Black, blue, and red jets of flame and curls of sulfurous smoke twisted up from the beast's scaly hide, indicating continued life, but it lay with its back unnaturally twisted. A dog in that position, Jim thought, would be dead.

A stray Zavuv descended on the fallen Hound, and Jim kicked it, smashing it against the wall.

"Jacob!" roared Belial. The Fallen surged through beetle soldiers towards the stairs. He nearly crushed Eddie, but as the beetles parted and ran, the guitarist was uncovered, and a split second before he would have been crushed flat by the giant's bulk, he rolled aside. "Jacob, wait!"

The Fallen reached the stairs.

Eddie rose to his feet and glared at Jim across the tempest and through an intermittent cloud of flies.

Jim turned away again. He leaped over Phthonos and ran into the passage.

Qayna waited for him, breathing hard. She held Gabriel's Horn in her hand just in case, but for the moment, at least, no one followed, not even the Zvuvim. The beetlelike minions must be doing their work.

The Marked Woman had a strange look on her face, insight mixed with curiosity. "How does this work?" was all she asked.

"What do you mean?"

She pointed with her gun back the way they had both come. "What stops just anyone from coming down this hall and interrupting the Council? And voting?"

"Besides the goons on the stairs?" Jim shrugged. It was a good question, really, and one he wished he had the answer to. A bad answer to the question could disrupt his plan now. "I don't know the details," he admitted. "I never cared until it was too late to ask, and no one has ever invaded Hell before. That I know of."

"There's some kind of warding, right?" she pressed.

"Something like that," he agreed. "I think this passage might not appear except for people who have a right to attend the Council."

"The passage appears for me."

"I don't know what your right is," he admitted. "Do you?"

Qayna lowered the pistol. "I came here once before. I was invited to come here again today. Does either of those count?"

"Maybe they both do." Jim turned and continued up the passage. Each *crack* and *boom* echoed down the hall from the entrance like a physical attack. "I think I have a right. I think I'm one of *them*."

Qayna was silent for a bit. "You mean the Infernal Princes. Do you not want to be one of them?"

Jim thought of the cannonball that had cut Elaine in half on the wall of Crannock Castle. He shook his head sadly. "I can't change my birth. But I'd like to rise above it."

"I'm not sure everything is quite what it seems. Maybe you don't *need* to rise above your birth. I know there's nobility in your father."

"Is there?" Jim laughed bitterly, thinking of the red-hot chains around Elaine's soul.

"Do you think he sees himself as evil? That he wants suffering?"

The passage ended in an arching span of stone, threading out ahead of them into the infinite up-and-down space of the Abyss. The catwalk ended against the side of a vast stalactite in an unrailed balcony and a tall door. Jim stopped and looked over his shoulder. "He at least permits it."

"More than *permits*. He inflicts it."

Jim snorted. "And you ask me if he wants it? What kind of game is this?"

It was Qayna's turn to shrug. "I don't know. A complex game, where not everything is as it seems and not everyone truly fights for the banner under which they march. Whatever game it is, I don't think I'm playing it anyway."

Jim stalked across the catwalk, shoving Sir John Horsham's sword into its scabbard at his belt as he went. "I'm done being a witness," he told her. "I'm done standing by. I'm going to act."

She didn't ask what he meant, and followed.

"Snocker," Jim said to one of the guards at the last door, and nodded to the other. "Chask."

Chask dragged his tongue off the floor and into his long, toothy mouth to titter a wordless reply. He ogled Qayna with mismatched eyes and tittered louder.

"Don't think I've forgotten you," Qayna told the door-keeper, and suddenly she had knives in both her hands. "And don't think you can touch."

Snocker clenched his four hands together innocently and bowed, turning to grapple with the door.

"Why is everything in your father's kingdom so ugly?" she asked.

"I don't know if it's ugly," Jim said, "so much as it's *homemade*."

"What, Heaven has all the factories?"

Jim nodded. "Which means that Hell has a punk aesthetic." Snocker got the door open and shuffled aside. The minion's perpetually bleeding knuckles had left orange smears on the stone of the door. "Do it yourself, you know? There's a reason rock and roll is Hell's music."

"I thought it was the rebellious attitude and the moral decadence." Qayna grinned.

"Nope." Jim walked into the Council Chamber. "Earth has the lock on moral decadence. Everyone in Hell toes the line. They have to."

He shut the door behind them.

The Council Chamber was immense. It seemed larger than the stalactite it occupied, though its preternaturally perfect acoustics meant participants had no difficulty hearing each other. The vast room was dominated by a circular table surrounded by Fallen-sized seats, one of which was larger than the others. The seats buzzed, hooted, and cracked with the shuffling, uneasy motion of their occupants. Not all the seats were occupied, but most were, and they were filled with the Princes. Jim saw Ezeq'el, her eyes downcast and liquid, rage-bubbling Semyaz, and Yamayol with flared taurine nostrils.

The single larger seat was the Morning Throne, and its occupant was Jim's father, Azazel. He looked across the Chamber at his son with unreadable eyes, and his posture was poised—relaxed but impeccable. He looked ready, at the slightest challenge, to crack his titan's whip and launch himself into the air with flapping wings. He had come prepared for a fight. A fight he had fought before, and a fight he had been expecting for an age.

Literally.

Qayna stopped at his shoulder. "Everyone?"

"Except the Princes," Jim conceded. "Of course."

"Call the question!" Semyaz screamed. Jim looked the pig-headed Infernal in his beady eyes and nodded. Semyaz gnashed his tusks back at Jim. The Fallen was furious but had no choice.

"Seconded," Jim said. His legs were tired, but not so tired that he couldn't leap from the floor to the outward-curving leg of the nearest chair, and from there into the seat itself. He stood rather than sitting, which made him nearly the same height as the Fallen ranged around the table. He looked around at them, recognizing them all, hating them for what they represented, hating himself because he was no different.

Across the table, Qayna similarly clambered into an empty chair.

"You don't know the question," sneered a Fallen whose head looked like it had originally come from or been inspired by a snail. *Jomjael*, Jim thought. A turtle shell crusted over her back, and each enormous hand had seven fingers, all drumming on the stone table.

"Don't I?" Jim stared at her until she flinched.

"Belial isn't here," she mumbled, looking down at her feet, which, Jim remembered though he couldn't see them, were horse's hooves. "There isn't a quorum."

"There's a quorum." Ezeq'el's eyes burned holes through Jim. Half of him wanted to laugh out loud, and the other half flinched, hoping the binding held.

Azazel nodded and thumped a heavy fist on the table. Jim forced himself to look at his father's face. He expected to see fear there, or at least uneasiness, but he didn't. He wasn't sure *what* he saw, but it might have been resignation. "The question has been called—"

"I am here!"

The new voice clanged like tearing iron—Belial. Jim forced himself not to turn and look, though the Fallen's voice came wreathed in the buzzing of flies. Too bad. Belial's followers would have nominated him and voted the same anyway, but Jim would have preferred to have one less vote for the octopoid Fallen.

"So am I!"

At this last, Jim couldn't help it. The Legate of Heaven stood in the door, and beside him was Eddie Marlowe. They were both battered, bloody, and crusted in pulverized stone. Each of them clutched one end of Azazel's hoof fragment. Behind them, Snocker and Chask closed the Chamber door, and the sound of the Zvuvim cut out again.

Eddie stared sourly at Jim. "You left me. I had no other choice."

Jim was impressed, and he guessed that Pilate had used sorcery and the hoof to somehow finesse the Chamber's wardings. Still, he shook his head; the stubborn guitar player had no idea what he was getting into.

"Belial," Azazel said smoothly, his voice rumbling warm and loud in the Chamber. "Welcome. You're expected."

The worm-eggplant-octopus Fallen heaved himself to the table like a drunk bellying up to the bar, knocking aside an unneeded seat. "I am here by right."

"I am here by cunning, ruthlessness, and sorcery," Pontius Pilate said. He let go of the hoof fragment and dragged himself awkwardly up into an oversized chair. No one helped him or spoke, and he settled himself carefully against the back of the seat, spreading out his red skirts and punching the dust out of them. "But I am here nevertheless, and I intend to vote."

"Legate." Azazel nodded.

Eddie Marlowe said nothing. He climbed into the last empty chair, pumped his shotgun to chamber a round, and furrowed his brows angrily at the entire gathering.

"The question has been called," Azazel said again. "Who shall rule in Hell? Nominations are open."

"Belial!" shrieked the snail-headed Fallen, Jomjael. Yamayol the bull snorted in disgust, and others of the Fallen hooted in derision. The cacophony was deafening.

Jim shot a look at the Marked Woman. She stood on her chair, a tiny, inconsequential cowgirl in her hat and duster. He didn't miss the fact, though, that her coat was brushed back behind her hip and one hand hung low beside her cursed pistol.

"Seconded," said the Legate of Heaven.

This is the deal Belial forged in the Queendom, Jim thought. He had made promises to the Legate and to Mab.

"Azazel." The nomination was hissed by a kilt-wrapped Fallen with the head of a serpent.

"Seconded." The voice belonged to Baraqyel, and the word made Jim notice him for the first time. The gatekeeper of Hell leaned in the corner of the room, blood running down his birdlike legs and matting his long white hair. He leaned on his spear like a broken man on a crutch. Jim felt a pang of compassion and fought to stay focused.

Azazel nodded. He looked tired, Jim thought, and old. The First Prince of Hell turned to look at Semyaz, no doubt expecting the same motions from his boar-faced rival that he always heard.

"I have a nomination," Semyaz growled, jutting his tusks at Azazel. He sounded like he was fighting a stomachache, and every word spattered yellow drool on the stone table in front of him.

Azazel didn't smile. "Let's hear it."

Semyaz snarled, low and guttural. "I nominate … Jacob bar Azazel."

A hiss ran around the table, turning heads as it went. Some stared at Azazel, some at Semyaz, and some at Jim.

"Seconded," Ezeq'el the centauress said sadly. The look on Azazel's face might have been shock.

Jim swallowed back a trembling feeling in his chest. "I move to close the nominations." He wondered whether he had enough support, even with all of Semyaz's crowd. He'd know soon enough.

Eddie stared at him across the table, uncertainty flashing in his eyes.

"Seconded," said Yamayol.

Adrian Pew's spell—his greatest spell, the one he hadn't understood that he was casting—had worked. The binding on the three Princes of the Fallen had held, and they had done as Jim had ordered.

So far.

"Very well." Azazel pounded the table again. He moved more slowly than usual, like an arthritic. "All in favor of closing the nominations."

A braying, screeching tumult of assent rang in the Chamber. Voting was by acclamation in the Council; the Fallen roared for the proposition they endorsed.

"All opposed."

Not a squeak. Eyes swiveled nervously about the room, astonished at the surprise attendees and the unexpected nominations; none of the Fallen wanted to add to the uncertainty they already felt and no doubt feared.

"Then we proceed to the vote."

Chapter Ten

The throng of beast-headed giants held its collective breath.

Jim looked at Eddie, the Legate, and Qayna.

Semyaz trembled, and his followers stared at him. Yamayol fumed, and Ezeq'el shed a single tear.

"Belial," Azazel said.

Belial himself emitted a sound like thunder, and so did all his followers. The Legate of Heaven raised his voice too, in a yell that was impossibly loud for a human throat. He was cheating, Jim thought, amplifying his voice with sorcery to make the acclaiming vote for Belial as loud as possible.

There was no point calling him on it. They had rules, and they all cheated.

"Azazel."

Another earsplitting roar. Baraqyel shot daggers at Jim with his eyes and pounded the butt of his spear on the floor as he yelled his approval. Azazel himself held his peace, and Jim squinted at his father. What was he doing?

"Jacob bar Azazel."

Semyaz howled the loudest, pounding the table before him, but Yamayol, Ezeq'el and all their faction threw in their animal screeches too. "Aye!" Jim shouted, and kicked the arm of the chair with his boot. Across the table, Eddie yelled something

Jim couldn't hear and fired his shotgun at the ceiling.

Jim and the guitar player locked eyes briefly, and Jim nodded his thanks.

"Gaaah!" Semyaz shouted as the clangor of the vote died away, smashing his own forehead into the tabletop. "Curse you, bar Azazel!"

"You started it," Jim growled, remembering Elaine enslaved inside the shadow of the now-dead Adrian Pew. "You never should have made promises you couldn't keep."

"Trickery!" Belial shouted, writhing against the table.

"You don't have a leg to stand on." Jim spat on the table in the beaked Fallen's direction. "Literally."

"A tie," Ezeq'el said. Her voice held a hopeful note, and she looked across the table at Azazel.

"Not everyone has voted." The Legate of Heaven reached inside his robes and pulled out a folded, wax-sealed sheet of paper. He set it slowly on the table in front of him and turned to look at the Marked Woman.

Qayna stood perfectly still, but under the shadow of her broad-brimmed hat, Jim would have sworn the tattooed curses on her face were writhing.

"Qayna?" Azazel prompted her.

She looked at Jim, then back at his father. Was she, Jim wondered, really just here to be a witness? "I don't have a vote."

"You do." Belial's beak ground out the words like a machine. "All present vote. You are here." He trembled, and the immense table rocked back and forth on contact with his shapeless body. "You know what you are offered."

Qayna hesitated. Jim forced himself to breathe calmly, feeling the muscles of his shoulders tense into knots hard as metal.

"What is offered ... if it is not, in fact, a trick ... is slavery," she finally said. "I'm not here to vote."

"No?" Belial shrieked, rising up and half falling across the edge of the table. The stone slab skidded sideways, knocking over several Fallen on the other side. "Then why are you here?"

Jim's own chair toppled over, and he leaped nimbly onto the table. Settling into a poised, ready stance, he drew his sword.

Just in case.

"I was invited." Qayna shrugged. "It was the only game in town."

Eddie pumped his shotgun to chamber another shell, watching Jim warily. "What the hell happens now? You know, forgive the pun …"

Belial's tentacles wiggled like a tub of live bait.

"There is another vote yet to be cast," said Baraqyel. The doorkeeper of Hell staggered forward from the corner, leaning on his spear. His grin was tired but wide—the grin of someone who has won a long and close race. Beside him, the snake-headed giant hissed in pleasure.

"Azazel." Ezeq'el looked up from the floor, face beaming.

All heads turned towards Lucifer, Moloch, the Accuser, the First Prince of Hell, the occupant of the Morning Throne since there had been a Morning Throne.

Azazel stood. Jim's father stretched his wings out wide and then folded them neatly against his shoulders. He rested both hands on the table.

"I am tired," he said simply, "and I think the time has come."

Many voices hissed uncertainly.

Ezeq'el's eyes opened wide. "Azazel?"

"No riddles!" Belial barked. "No evasions! Vote, or there is no Satan!"

A faint smile curled on Azazel's face. "No Satan?" he asked. His cool eyes traveled around the table, touching on each attendee. They lingered, Jim thought, on Qayna and Eddie. They passed over the Legate without hesitation and came to rest on Jim. "What would that be like?"

"Don't you remember?" Jim asked his father. In his own mind's eye, he saw the spires of Ainok, the grand spiral of its canals, the glittering white stone and dark wood.

Azazel nodded and looked again at Qayna. "I remember," he said. "I remember … perhaps too much."

"Vote!" Belial squealed.

Semyaz pounded the table again in mute rage.

The other Fallen stared, uncertain.

Azazel nodded and looked again at his son. Jim tightened his grip on his sword. His father's hoof fragment lay forgotten in the corner; he prepared himself to leap for it. He could live to fight again another day, return to his original plan. He knew now that it was possible to free the damned, and he could—

"Jacob bar Azazel."

Jim heard his own name come from his father's lips, and it felt like the six syllables took an eon to pronounce.

His head swam. His knees buckled, and he fought to stand.

"Nooooooo!" Semyaz bellowed, and hurled himself forward onto the table.

Jim was stunned. He wanted to move aside, but he was exhausted, surprised, and off balance. Semyaz rushed at him like a train with a boar's head, roaring and slashing with ragged talons.

He had done it, Jim thought. He had taken the Morning Throne, and now he was going to die.

Bang! Bang! Bang!

Semyaz's claws missed, but his body plowed into Jim like a bus. Jim was swept away under a ton of pig's head and eagle's wings, off the table, and he smashed against the wall. He lost his grip on his sword. Blinding flashes of light filled his vision, and his breath was squeezed from him. Semyaz writhed on him in all his bulk like an elephant having an epileptic fit.

Bang! Bang! Bang!

A final shudder.

Bang!

Stillness. Jim felt very, very small and flat.

This was death, then.

But Semyaz lay on him like a fallen log, not finishing his attack.

When air returned to Jim's lungs and the room stopped spinning, he felt and smelled hot blood pouring over him. Not his own; Semyaz's blood. And he saw that the former Prince of the Fallen had three neat bullet holes in his temple.

"Seven trumpets," someone murmured. He wasn't sure who.

He heard padding soles of combat boots on the floor, and then Eddie Marlowe dragged him out from under the dead giant. Jim stood awkwardly and tried not to show the weakness and pain he felt. Qayna stood in the corner, pistol still in her hand.

"Qayna," Azazel said in a calm voice. "You have broken the peace of the Infernal Council."

"You call that *peace*?" Eddie muttered, but he hunkered down at Jim's side and didn't draw attention to himself.

"Will you punish me, Lucifer?" she asked. She raised her eyebrows as she spoke, like she was daring Azazel to do his worst. "Will you kill me?"

"It is not my place to punish you." Azazel stepped away from the Morning Throne. "And I am no longer Lucifer."

The Fallen were silent.

Jim stared in uncomprehending shock.

"Jacob bar Azazel," his father said, "Firstfruits of Ainok the Free. You are Moloch, greatest among the Princes of the Fallen. Take your Throne."

Jim staggered to the Morning Throne. It was a simple gray seat, hewn from the natural stone of the Chamber, and he kept his eye fixed on it as if the image itself would hold him up. When he reached it, he lurched up its steps and collapsed onto the stone, warmed by his father's immense body.

Energy rushed through him.

Jim gasped, looking up at his father standing beside and above him. He couldn't decipher Azazel's expression. Jim tingled. He felt alive and strong. The Throne quivered and sighed beneath him like a living thing, and a rush of sound like tumbling waters filled his ears. In the rush, he thought he heard a million cries, a million whispers, and a million peals of laughter, none of it originating in the Council Chamber.

He sat upright and looked around the table.

Eddie and Qayna stood in the corner beside the corpse of Semyaz. They looked tiny, and their guns looked even tinier.

The Legate furrowed his brows at Jim, his folded paper swept off the table and hidden away again. Yamayol sat back in his seat, stunned. Ezeq'el and Baraqyel wept openly. Belial gnashed his beak and trembled.

No one spoke.

Azazel turned and walked away from the Morning Throne. He hesitated near Qayna for a moment, but neither of them said anything. In the open door, he stopped and turned.

"There is one other item of business," Jim said.

He hadn't planned this, but he saw now that it was possible. He saw that the Princes would vote for it—enough of them, anyway, for the motion to pass. His accession was the thing that would make them accept it—they would choose formless, unknown opportunity for their ambitions over doubt about what Jim's rule would entail.

And he had some votes in his pocket already.

"Name it," Yamayol huffed. The bull-headed Fallen gripped the edge of the table, his massive knuckles white.

"I move to disband the Council. Free us all. Empty Hell."

Stunned disbelief on giant faces.

"Is this wise?" the Legate of Heaven asked, frowning.

Azazel started forward. "But the damned ..."

"I free them," Jim snarled.

"You can't." All eyes stared, shifting back and forth between Jim and his father.

"But I *do*!"

Jim slammed his fists on the arms of the Morning Throne and willed it. With the force of his mind, and with the energy in the seat beneath him, he threw open the gates of Hell and cast all its minions and prisoners out. He seized Hell in his mind and bent it against itself to break it. He felt power flow through him like a hurricane through a bottle's neck, stripping stone off the canyon walls and flesh and life out of his chest. The rushing in his ears grew to a ringing yell. Pain wracked him, and he gritted his teeth against it, staring at his father.

KRAAANGGG!

The Council Chamber split down the middle as if struck by a hammer. A continuous crack snapped into being all along the floor, two walls, and the ceiling, and one half of the room dropped six inches. The table groaned loudly and then it, too, split along the middle and collapsed.

Far away, outside the Council Chamber, clangs, booms, crashes.

He didn't know what he'd expected, but his expectations hadn't been that ... loud. Jim sucked in air. Already tired and pounded by Semyaz, he felt drained of vitality by the Throne now, too.

Azazel bowed his head and shoulders. "I didn't know you intended this."

"I *didn't*." Jim stood slowly. His knees trembled and he looked over the room. "Now get out. All of you."

He didn't watch them go. He couldn't; he was too broken. He held himself erect between the Throne and the table, the departing Fallen a blur before his eyes. When the Chamber had emptied out, he collapsed back into the Morning Throne. This time, it had no energy to give him. The rushing-water sound of voices was gone. He closed his eyes and felt physical comfort in the cool stone.

"What the hell, Jim?"

Eddie. Jim opened his eyes. The guitar player and Qayna the Marked Woman were the only ones left in the room with him. They looked like children next to the oversized seats of the Infernal Council, or dolls.

"This wasn't quite what I planned," Jim said weakly. He felt smashed flat.

"No shit. It wasn't what I planned, either."

The Left Hand still rested on the guitar player. As Jim looked at him, Eddie's bad eye slid sideways, and he shuddered.

"I ..." Jim gripped the arms of the seat. He had freed the damned, hadn't he? He had meant to free Eddie. "Hold on."

"You owe me." Eddie stared at Jim fiercely, sawed-off shotgun trembling in his hand. "You owe Mike and Twitch. You didn't get here alone, damn you. Hell, you owe Adrian, if you can find the poor son of a bitch."

Jim closed his eyes and tried to feel his way into the Morning Throne. It lay inert under him, cool and lifeless.

"Jim?"

He opened his eyes. Eddie's face was full of blame, but Qayna's was curious.

"You're Jacob," she said.

Jim stood, nodding.

"I killed you," she continued.

He staggered away from the Throne and towards the door. "I died," he admitted. "I wouldn't have said you were responsible."

"Jim?" Eddie called, and they both followed him out.

Jim lurched because he couldn't run. Snocker and Chask were gone, and the bridge connecting the Council Chamber to the rest of Hell lay silver-lit and cold across the Abyss. The crack that had split the Chamber ran along the bridge as well, and as Jim and the others reached the far side of the slender span, the bridge finally cracked. Jim didn't look back, but the immense crashing sound of the Council Chamber's stalactite slipping into the Abyss and taking the bridge with it chilled him.

Jim half-expected Zvuvim to harry their path, but the flies were gone. Emerging from the arched hallway, he found Phthonos. The Hellhound still lay whimpering, its back twisted. It looked up at Jim with mournful eyes, and Jim staggered past.

In the rubble he found Elaine.

Only one of her, standing, and with her chain still wrapped about her. No sign of her father.

As he stumbled down the stairs, Mike rose up to intercept him. "Hey, *maricón*, when the hell are we getting outta here?" Twitch lay on the ground beside Mike, staring up with battered eyes.

Jim ignored them. "Elaine!" he called.

She whimpered. "I would not complain, love," she said. "But I hurt."

Jim grabbed the end of the chain and gasped at its heat. He willed it to fall from her, struggling at the same time to unwrap it.

"No," she moaned.

"Jim!"

Eddie and Qayna arrived on the stairs at his back. Jim turned, trembling, seeing blame and anger in their eyes. Eddie had again picked up his father's hoof clipping, forgotten by those who had chased so eagerly after it in the chaos of the Council's meeting. Forgotten by Jim.

"I know!" Jim screamed, wiping blinding sweat from his face. "I screwed up!"

"Yeah?" Eddie's face was ashen.

"I thought I could save you." Jim sank to his knees, wasted. "I thought I saw a chance to grab the Throne from my father. I *did* see it. I thought I could free you—free you all. But the Throne just opened the doors and let everyone out. It didn't save anyone."

"That wasn't our plan," Eddie growled. "There was no Throne in our plan. Our plan was trade the hoof to your dad for what we wanted, and if that didn't work, use the hoof to force him. When the hell did you get big ideas?"

"Kansas City." Jim tried to stand but couldn't. The size of his failure overwhelmed him.

"Semyaz and the others. They agreed to vote for you."

"I forced them. Adrian forced them."

Eddie sat on the steps and sighed. "Now what?"

"Help me," Elaine whimpered. Her chain rattled on the floor.

"It must be possible." Jim looked up. "I know it's possible to remove the Left Hand."

"Yeah?" Eddie looked skeptical. "How do you know that?"

"Mike." Jim pointed. "I don't know how he did it, but he lost the Left Hand since he came in here."

The both looked at the bass player.

Mike scowled and snorted. "*Concha de tu madre, pendejo.* Why the hell do you think I'm *Mike?*"

Eddie frowned. "Sounds like he ain't gonna be much help. Where does that leave us?" He shook the hoof fragment. "Your father again? Chicago?"

Jim struggled to his feet again. He felt tired and very, very old. He looked at Elaine.

She groaned. "Help me."

Jim sobbed. "I can't."

Eddie looked away, embarrassed or disgusted.

"They came for your beat-up friend." Mike jerked a thumb at Twitch and brandished his pistol. "Me and the horse chased 'em off."

Jim looked at Twitch. "Who came?"

"Mab," the fairy croaked. "And her Rangers. The Mare of Diomedes frightened them off, but they'll be back. My exile is over, and I've been condemned to death."

Jim shook his head, feeling beaten. "And Raphael?"

"I last saw him fighting off a Hellhound and a Baal Zavuv," Eddie said. "He didn't look too happy that the old guy made a deal with me."

"What deal?"

Eddie fixed one eye sternly on Jim while the other slid off in random directions. "You think you got a right to know?"

Jim sagged. "No. And it doesn't matter."

Twitch closed its eyes slowly. "Death might be better than this, don't you think?"

Eddie whistled through his teeth slowly. "No deal," he said. "Or anyway, no deal that isn't over and done. I shared the hoof with him, he got me through the door."

"Help me," Elaine said again.

"I can't free you," Jim admitted. "I thought I could do it. I'm sorry. Maybe ... maybe my father."

"She's not asking to be freed." Qayna finished refilling the clip of her famous pistol and snapped it back into place.

Jim turned to Elaine again. His love's face burned, and the smell of her roasting flesh and melting hair stung his nostrils. "Help me, James."

Jim stood uncertain. "How?"

"She needs you to punish her." Jim wasn't sure whose voice had spoken. He was too distracted by the sight of Elaine before him, burning and crying.

"No." His lips felt numb.

Elaine groaned.

"I can free her. I …" Jim looked about him at the rubble of his father's mansions. "Help!" he hollered, and his voice echoed back at him without mercy.

"James …"

"I'll do it."

He grabbed the dangling end of Elaine's chain with both hands. The iron was hot, and his hands burned, but he held tight, ignoring the stench of his own flesh scorching along with hers.

"Please …"

He pulled. The force of his arms jerked a sob out of his own chest and he thought he felt her bones breaking, but the sound that slipped from Elaine Canning's beautiful lips was a grunt of relief.

Jim held the chain and wept.

"How do we get out of here?" Eddie asked later. The pain broke Jim's sense of time, and he wondered how long he'd left the guitar player standing there.

Jim stood. "I can't come with you."

Eddie's face was hard. "Fine. Show me the way out."

Jim nodded. "I'll lead you. One last time."

"One last time."

He dragged Elaine with him through the empty caverns of Hell. She resisted, and sighed and moaned with relief every time he had to yank to pull her along with him. At some point in the dimming red darkness of the vaults, he began to sing.

A cold north wind is blowing
Down along the range
The man with the banjo and the three-legged mule
Drifts across the plain
The snow piles up in lonely humps
But you won't hear him complain
He just thinks of her and how
With a song of unspeakable sorrow
He broke her heart
He broke her heart
He broke her heart

It was one of his, written for her during the cold nights of the '49 Rush.

Every step was agony for Jim's body and soul, and neither the song nor their arrival at the gates gave any solace.

The doors hung on one hinge each. Myriad claw and bite marks in the metal told the tale of the doors' opening.

"What's out there?" Eddie asked, thumbing more shells into his shotgun and stuffing Azazel's hoof fragment inside his torn green jacket as he caught up. He sniffed and wiped one eye, and Jim wondered dully if he was emotional. Behind him, the Marked Woman led her horse, carrying Twitch on it. Mike walked muttering to one side.

Jim shook his head and shrugged. "I'm not the doorkeeper. *Outside* is out there. It could be the ruins of Ainok, it could be Missouri, I don't know."

Eddie peered through the shattered doors. "Missouri, huh?" A hot wind blew smoke in through the ruined gate. "Missouri's changed since I last saw it."

Jim felt nothing but the pain in his hands and the hammering of his heart. He pulled on Elaine's bindings and she moaned gratefully. "Yeah?"

"Yeah," Eddie said, and he pumped his shotgun. "It's on fire." The guitar player turned over his shoulder and called to the others. "Come on, then. I'm still damned and I still aim to do something about it. This ain't over yet."

Jim stared after the broken remains of his rock band as they staggered out into the burning night in the company of Qayna, the Marked Woman. Then he saw that Elaine cringed back from the light and the heat.

"Come," he whispered to her, and pulled again on the searing chains that bound her … the chains, he realized, that bound them both.

He led her back through Hell with the last of the dying Infernal light, singing.

> *The drunks are up the gangplank*
> *Staggering pair by pair*
> *The woman with too many late nights in her eyes*

Flips a final chair
She knows the flood is coming soon
But she just shakes out her hair
She thinks of him and how
With a song of unspeakable sorrow
He broke her heart
He broke her heart
He broke her heart

As the red glow finally faded into nothing, he saw a glimmer ahead. Picking their way through rubble and over corpses, Jim brought his lady love past the Audience Hall to an unrailed balcony where once he had confronted his father.

The Abyss was still brilliant with light.

Elaine moaned piteously, and he pulled the chain harder.

"I love you, James," she whimpered.

"I love you, too."

The smell of the burning flesh of his own hands clogged Jim's nostrils, and the searing pain nearly knocked him to his knees. He dragged Elaine Canning closer to him and held her, feeling the burn across his chest as well as in his palms.

He looked up the endless tunnel of light and felt tears begin to fill his eyes.

What had he done?

About the Author

D.J. Butler (Dave) is a novelist living in the Rocky Mountain northwest. His training is in law, and he worked as a securities lawyer at a major international firm and in house at two multinational semiconductor manufacturers before taking up writing fiction.

Dave writes speculative fiction for all audiences. In addition to his steampunk, urban fantasy, and science fiction novels published with WordFire Press, his books are published by Knopf (*The Kidnap Plot*) and Baen (*Witchy Eye*, forthcoming).

Dave is a lover of language and languages, a guitarist and self-recorder, and a serious reader. He is married to a powerful and clever woman and together they have three devious children.

Read about Dave's writing projects at: http://davidjohnbutler.com.

IF YOU LIKED ...

If you liked *The Good Son,* you might also enjoy:

Quincy J. Allen
Chemical Burn
Blood Ties

Josh Vogt
Enter the Janitor
Maids of Wrath

OTHER WORDFIRE PRESS TITLES BY D.J. BUTLER

City of the Saints

Crecheling

Rock Band Fights Evil

Hellhound on My Trail,

Snake Handlin' Man,

Crow Jane,

Devil Sent the Rain

Our list of other WordFire Press authors and titles is always growing. To find out more and to see our selection of titles, visit us at:

wordfirepress.com

BLACK AMAZON OF MARS

AN ERIC JOHN STARK

ADVENTURE

BY

LEIGH BRACKETT

VERTVOLTA PRESS
REDISCOVERY
Edition